SWITZERLAND: *"The OGPU discourages the resignation of its men!" remarked an agent of the Soviet secret service. What he did not say was, that its method of discouragement is both effective and complete, as the case of Ignace Reiss proves conclusively.*

THE OGPU MARKS THE SPOT

By

Renè Benoit

HAPPILY whistling the air of an old folk tune, the Swiss peasant lad, starting his ascent to one of the hospices on the Lausanne-Chambland road, stopped dead in his tracks, the tune dying abruptly on his puckered lips. For a long moment he gazed in horrified fascination at the gruesome object lying in his path, then turned and ran, screaming, down the mountainside.

" . . . his—his h-head is almost off!" the boy stammered incoherently when he reached his father's side, the color of his face matching the fallen snow. "And—there's blood!—blood everywhere!"

The boy's father immediately notified the gendarmerie of nearby Lausanne, and six troopers were sent post-haste to the scene. When the spot described by the terrified youth was reached even the gendarmes, made callous by long experience with death and violence, were sickened.

Lying in the blood-drenched snow, twisted in a grotesque posture, was the body of a man of about 40. He had been riddled with bullets which, upon examination, were found to have been fired from a sub-machine gun.

So many of the deadly pellets had entered the man's neck that the head was almost severed from the torso. Police were reminded of gangster killings in the most gory American tradition.

But this was peaceful Switzerland! Who would use a Tommy-gun in the orderly and tidy little Republic? The gendarmes scratched their heads and swore softly. Then, quickly coming to the business at hand, they spread out a canvas and gingerly placed the man's stiff, cold body upon it. Hastening down the mountain, they drove back to Lausanne and to the small morgue behind the Palais de la Justice. There the authorities launched their investigation.

THE BODY found on the morning of September 4th, 1937 was well-dressed, although lacking an overcoat—a garment required in that part of the country even in September. Judging from the condition of the man's dress, fingernails and shoes, the police deduced the victim was a business man or moderate well-to-do tourist.

But unquestionably he was not a Swiss, on the basis of the external evidence.

Methodically, the police proceeded to go through his clothes.

In the man's inside coat-pocket was a wallet which enclosed a Czech passport, issued to one Hans Eberhardt. There was also an unused railroad ticket from Paris to Lausanne. That was all that could be found in his clothes.

The police soon discovered that the passport was of no value as a clue. They had heard of "Hans Eberhardt" before in various anonymous letters to the gendarmerie. These messages had described a man by that name as a smuggler of narcotics and somewhat more vaguely, "an adventurer."

Authorities, after an exhaustive inquiry, satisfied themselves that no "Hans Eberhardt" existed in fact, and that the passport was a forgery which had been planted on the body to befuddle investigators.

The following day, however, detectives obtained their first break in the case. A highly nervous woman, about the same age as the dead man, appeared at the morgue and asked to see the body. She said she had read of its discovery in the Geneva newspapers.

When she saw the condition of the corpse, she fainted. A police surgeon revived her. To the Swiss *juge d'instruction,* or examining magistrate, she identified herself as the widow of the bullet-ridden man.

"My husband's name," she said between sobs, "was Ignace Reiss. The passport you found is, of course, false. His own must have been removed after his—death.

"He was of Polish origin, and a master spy of the OGPU, the Soviet secret-service. For several months he had been on a special mission to France and Holland, and while waiting for him to wind up his affairs I have been living in a village near here."

FICTION HOUSE PRESS
PRESENTS

WORLD DETECTIVE CASES

January 1939
Vol. 1, No. 1

This reprint edition is a facsimile of the original digest magazine. Variations in printing and quality can be attributed to the original magazine which was printed on rough woodpulp paper.

ISBN 978-1-64720-251-4

www.FictionHousePress.com
fictionhousepress@gmail.com

The magistrate asked: "What motive, Madame, might there be for murdering your husband?"

Hate blazing from her eyes, Madame Reiss replied, "He was not murdered. He was assassinated!"

"By whom? For what reason? Tell us what you know."

But with the sudden flare-up of fury, the victim's wife shrank into a shell of silence, and could not be induced to elaborate on her charge that her husband had been slain for political reasons. To the police it was clear the woman was in fear of her life if she talked.

The police had no grounds on which to hold her, and her papers were in order. They released Madame Reiss, but ordered her to remain at the disposition of the authorities.

THE positive identification of the victim was of some aid, but not much. All the police knew thus far was that a man named Ignace Reiss had been filled with lead from a sub-machine gun, that he had come from Paris, that he had a wife living in the district, and that he was an OGPU agent assigned to a special mission in France and Holland.

Not a single clue to the killers had been found at the scene of the assassination. If an automobile had been used in the murder, the light snow had obliterated the tire tracks. Nor were there signs of footprints.

But two days later, on September 7th, there came the second break in the mystery. The manager of the Hotel de la Paix in Lausanne reported, as required ! law, that two guests, who had registered there on September 3rd, had failed to return the following day after spending the night and had not paid their bill. They had left their luggage, however.

The two guests were a man and a woman, and they had arrived at the hotel in a car driven by the man.

Police fine-combed the luggage of the pair, who had taken adjoining rooms. They found a mass of articles, papers and photographs. The woman was disclosed as being Gertrude Schildbach, neé Neigebauer, who was prone to hide her rather marked good-looks behind heavy spectacles.

She had been a well-known Communist Party member in Germany, where she was born, according to records the Swiss police found in the hotel, but she had fled at about the time the Nazis charged Communists with setting the Reichstag ablaze. Thereafter she had worked for the OGPU in Paris and, more recently, in Rome.

Madame Reiss after repeated questioning, finally admitted that she knew Frau Schildbach, and that her husband had known and trusted her implicitly for more than 20 years. Besides, the widow said, she had not the slightest reason to suspect the German woman Communist of complicity in any plot to assassinate her husband.

Frau Schildbach's companion, police next learned, was a 38-year-old Frenchman named Francois Rossi, whom police records disclosed as having occasionally used the alias of Roland Abbia. From a passport photograph found in his room, police judged him to be a fairly "anti-social" member of society.

They were correct, for he also was a member of the OGPU, and his field of activity was Monte Carlo.

By degrees, now the first pieces of the puzzle were falling into place, despite the setback administered by Madame Reiss when she convinced police that she had no knowledge of Rossi, alias Abbia.

As yet the authorities were still a long way from linking the assassination with Frau Schildbach and her chauffeur-companion. Certainly there was something suspicious about the pair and the manner of their leaving the hotel. But the fact that she was a Communist was not necessarily a clue, nor evidence against her.

For many years, since and before the World War, Switzerland has been a haven for Russian revolutionaries and Communists. It had been a sanctuary for Lenin and Trotsky, who engineered the revolution in Russia from their Alpine haven.

OVERNIGHT one of the investigators suddenly realized that he and his colleagues had overlooked what might prove to be a valuable clue to the whereabouts of the missing couple. The history of criminal detection is replete in instances of investigators ignoring clues because they lie right beneath their noses. So it had proved at the present stage of this case.

What was the license number of the car in which the Schildbach woman and Rossi arrived at the Hotel de la Paix!

Swiss cantonal law, like *arrondissement* ordinances in neighboring France, require traveling motorists to register their license numbers, just as they must report to the authorities with their passports and identity cards. It proved a simple matter for police to summon the hotel concierge, who in turn referred to the ledgers he kept for the prefecture.

Now seemingly again hot on the trail, the police learned that the machine, an expensive foreign-make, had been rented August 30th from a garage in Berne by a woman who gave her name as Renata Steiner. The garage owner declared she had come to him, explaining she was a tourist, had paid a substantial deposit and driven away with the car.

On the afternoon of this discovery, the Steiner woman returned to the garage and explained that she had lent the car for a few hours to friends. Had it been returned?

No, it had not been returned. "And moreover, mademoiselle," a police officer told her as she was about to leave the garage in an obvious hurry, "you are under arrest!"

But la Steiner, an opulent and patrician brunette, was not to be intimidated. She shrugged her attractive shoulders, and refused to say a word, save that she had let a trio of friends have the machine for a few hours, precisely as she had told the people at the garage.

Police locked her up to see whether a few hours' solitude might make her more articulate.

The clues thus far seemed pertinent and promising, but the authorities had yet to link Schildbach, Rossi and Steiner to the machine-gunning of Reiss. As police were again interrogating the widow, striving to learn something of her slain husband's habits, friends and activities, a station attendant in distant Geneva reported an interesting find.

The discovery—which definitely proved the missing link in the murder conspiracy—was that of a car, abandoned in the square facing the principal railroad station of Geneva.

Item 1: The tonneau was spattered with blood.

Item 2: The license was that of the machine rented by Fraulein Steiner on August 30th at Berne.

Item 3: In the car was found a light overcoat, bearing the label of a Madrid tailor, which Madame Reiss identified as having belonged to her husband.

The finding of the car, its condition and contents, almost conclusively implicated the Schildbach woman and Rossi, the two OGPU agents, with the assassination. Even Reiss' widow, after recovering from her shock, was all but persuaded that her husband's confidante of years, was guilty.

The Steiner girl, however, would admit nothing. If murder had been committed in the machine, she said, it had been done by persons stealing it. Police continued to keep her in jail when she steadfastly refused to reveal the names of the friends to whom she had lent it.

The Swiss police were making progress, but they had not apprehended the Schildbach agent and her male companion. The fact that the machine had been found near the railroad station suggested that the couple had fled Switzerland by train.

Two Lausanne detectives were sent to Paris to get whatever information they could of the OGPU set-up in France. There they worked with a number of stool-pigeons and with members of the so-called Political Secret Service of the Third French Republic.

Further to aid them, Madame Reiss consented at last to tell the

Swiss and French authorities all she knew of her late husband—his work, career and companions—provided she were guaranteed police protection day and night, as she was in terror of a fate similar to his. The police agreed she had grounds for her fears.

Over a period of five months, French and Swiss operatives traced down all the bizarre ramifications of the conspiracy to assassinate Reiss. It was painstaking and dangerous work. When they were finished with their labors, they had learned that Reiss had been "liquidated," just as the more celebrated Nicolai Bukharin, Zinoviev, Rykov, Piatakov and Rakovsky had been "purged" somewhere in the depths of the multiple-cellered Kremlin.

The difference was that, in the case of Reiss the Soviet Commissariat for Home Affairs, which controls the dread OGPU, had boldly reached beyond its borders, and taken one of its agents for a "ride" in a country hundreds of miles from the Soviet Union.

None was supposed to know, however, that the Stalin internal purge would be extended abroad. The reprisals outside the Soviet Union were to be made to appear as commonplace murders, of no political significance.

When the police of two nations closed their wide-spread inquiry, they had in their files the almost unbelievable story of Reiss, his background, why he was ordered to be executed, and the closing chapter—how he met his death on a windblown mountain in Switzerland. In these records are intrigue, chicanery, double-crossing and attempted murder by poison.

IGNACE REISS was the son of a middle-class family of Cracow, Poland. He was born January 1, 1899. By the time he reached high-school he had lost patience with what he considered the *bourgeois* outlook of his parents, and was ready material for the revolutionary elements in Poland, then a part of Czarist Russia, which sought recruits even among pupils in the secondary school.

Parental authority forced Reiss to matriculate at the University of Vienna to study law. But, unknown to his father and mother, these studies were merely a blind for his activities as a highly resourceful and intrepid member of the Communist Party.

He was a sincere believer in the tenets of Marxism, and almost totally without personal ambition. He was convinced that the wrongs suffered by his native Poland could only be righted by Communism. With Trotsky, he advocated world revolution.

To that end the young Reiss was ready to give his life. And, because of this fanatical idealism, other and less selfless members of the Communist Party recognized his usefulness: he was ready to do what opportunist members of the Party dared not do.

His first major assignment was a mission to conduct underground activity in Poland by which was meant the organization of students and other young revolutionaries into "cells." This was in 1920, after Poland had regained her independence and Russia had liquidated the Czarist family.

But the twenty - one - year - old Communist overplayed his hand in his eagerness to effect a revolution. The Warsaw authorities nabbed him and he was sentenced to five years in prison after refusing to reveal his co-conspirators. He kept silent even after an hour's subjection to the modern equivalent of the medieval rack.

On a technicality he was granted a new trial, after six months, and admitted to bail. He fled across the frontier to Moscow and arrived in Red Square, a hardened, ingenious, courageous revolutionary.

The Comintern recognized his potential usefulness and assigned him to Germany where, in 1923-26, he was an under-cover agitator in the Ruhr—an exceedingly dangerous assignment. The next year he landed in Vienna. Twenty-four hours later he was once more in jail.

In another year he was free and en route to Moscow. And in 1928, for "meritorious services to the proletarian revolution," Reiss was awarded the Order of the Red Banner, one of the most highly prized decorations by Communists.

By this time the OGPU had developed into an organization even more efficient than its predecessor, the fearful Czarist Cheka. Its director, I. Yezhov, with the approval of Dictator Stalin, determined to send secret agents abroad not only for purposes of espionage, but also to check on the activities of Soviet diplomatic envoys and consular officials some of whom had reportedly sold out to the capitalistic countries to which they were accredited. Many of these, on information dug up by Reiss and other OGPU agents, later were ordered to return to Moscow, on one pretext or another, and disappeared in the extensive purge.

IN 1928 Reiss was given secret assignments in Eastern Europe, and the year following saw him in an administrative post with the OGPU at Moscow headquarters. Himself incorruptible, he would tolerate no disloyalty from other Communist officials, but about this time he began to feel that Stalin had scuttled Communism for a program of executions directed at making him Dictator.

Reiss was gratified when Yezhov, because of Reiss' linguistic ability and grasp of German and Spanish affairs, dispatched him to Western Europe in another administrative — although undercover — capacity. The work was risky, particularly because it exposed him to charges of treason by other agents jealous of his authority abroad.

Thus Reiss never knew, working in Paris, Amsterdam, Berlin or Madrid, when he would be summoned to Moscow, or what would be his fate on his return.

In 1936 he concluded that Stalin was effecting the disintergration of the party by his sanguinary program of blood-thirsty executions. To Reiss and many other revolutionaries, the so-called "trials" were farcical. He knew that many of his comrades had faced the firing-squad, or had been exiled to Siberia.

Once his mind was made up, there was no turning back for Reiss. He determined to give up his life-work which, he felt now, made him no less than an accessory to murder. He would resign from the party, after first warning men whom he knew were marked for execution.

Accordingly, in 1937, he took tremendous risks in making contact in Paris with the anti-Stalin (Trotsky) Communists. He sent them this word of caution:

> "The decision has been taken to resort to all means against you. Understand me correctly when I write—*All means*. All your men are in danger!"

Treachery? Perhaps — in the eyes of the Moscow Comintern. But not to Reiss. He could endure no more the successive execution of men whom he knew personally to be loyal party workers, men with whom he had shared prison cells and constant danger. Such men were only disloyal, in his eyes, to Stalin's plans to concentrate all power in his own hands.

He dispatched the warning to the Trotskyites in the spring of 1937, a fact since corroborated by Trotsky. When he returned to his small room that evening at the Hotel Pajou, at 20 rue de Roche, the clerk nodded at the tall, athletic Russian and wondered why the quiet, pleasant-mannered guest should look so preoccupied and upset.

Once he had dispatched the letter of warning, Reiss never knew at what moment he might be shot in the back or, en route home, be stabbed to death in one of the dark narrow alleys of Paris. Little wonder he appeared distraught that night.

HIS next step was a stumble, and the first of several that led him to his end on that distant Swiss mountain road. He felt obligated to make his resignation known to Moscow together with the reasons prompting him. At his desk in the hotel room—knowing the added risks he was incurring—he wrote a letter to the Central Committee of the Communist Party of the U.S.S.R.

It was dated July 17, 1937, and it read:

> "Up to now I have been with you. From now on, our roads part. He who can keep silent at this hour becomes an accomplice of Stalin and a traitor to the cause of labor and Socialism. One must not deceive oneself. Truth will find its way. The day of judgment is near, much nearer than the gentlemen in the Kremlin think. Nothing will be forgiven. History is a rigorous mistress, and the 'genius of our leadership, the Father of Nations, the Sun of Socialism' (*titles popularly accorded Stalin. Ed.*) will have to render an accounting for all his deeds."

When he signed the bitter resignation, he also signed his death warrant.

The next day he phoned Lydia Grozovskaya, an attractive Georgian agent working in Paris as an undercover "postoffice" for OGPU communications. Her duties consisted of forwarding mail to Moscow Headquarters that could not be entrusted safely to the regular channels. Reiss had known Lydia many years, and trusted her no less than he did Gertrude Schildbach.

They met in a cellar cafe.

"Lydia," he told the woman, "get this immediately to Moscow! By the underground route. Can I trust you?"

"Of course, Comrade! Why do you look so worried? Take heart!"

They said farewell affectionately, and Reiss returned to the Hotel Pajou. By the secret channels, it would take his letter of resignation from three to four days to reach Moscow. In that time, surely, he could pack, summon his wife from Switzerland to Paris, and flee to South America.

He would be gone before the OGPU could reach him.

Or so Reiss thought.

Lydia Grozovskaya betrayed his without a qualm. She took the letter post-haste to her superior, Mikhail Spiegelglass, the acting director of the foreign secret service of the OGPU, then in the French capital on an important mission.

That evening, while Reiss was still in his hotel-room, Spiegelglass telephoned Moscow. The order he received was covered by two words:

"Liquidate Reiss!"

Thus instructed, Spiegelglass called an immediate conference. Among those summoned were Lydia Grozovskaya and her husband, a member of the Soviet Trade Mission named Beletsky, and another, thought to have been the attractive Renata Steiner.

A plan was swiftly devised to kidnap Reiss. According to the Swiss authorities, who reported that "the crime was committed by agents of the OGPU acting upon orders of the Kremlin," the proposed kidnappers and assassins were authorized to spend $15,000 to eliminate Reiss.

A few minutes after the meeting broke up, the phone rang in Reiss' room. When he answered it, there was no one at the other end of the wire. This happened three times.

Reiss understood. He fled the hotel through the kitchen, without so much as a toothbrush. Once in the street, he tarried only long enough to mail a letter to a Paris friend, giving his probable destination as Amsterdam where, he wrote, that he would stay with another friend, a former deputy named Sneevlit.

A few minutes after the letter was received by Reiss' "friend," its message was fully known to Spiegelglass.

The man-hunt was on in earnest.

TWO OGPU agents in Paris, named Ducomet and Zadek, chartered a plane, hoping to reach Amsterdam before Reiss. Others sought him in Chamonix, whence there is a mountain pass across the Swiss frontier. Meanwhile, agents were watching all the trains leaving for Holland at the Gare de Nord in Paris.

But there was no sign of Reiss. Infuriated, the OGPU agents continued their hunt, day and night.

Reiss, meanwhile, made another tragic blunder. He had never been near Amsterdam: he had mailed the letter solely to mislead his pursuers. He had purchased a railroad ticket to Lausanne but, afraid to use it, he made his way to the Swiss city by a circuituous route, traveling in buses, hayracks and sometimes a-foot, expecting to rejoin his wife.

In Lausanne he met his old confidante, Gertrude Schildbach. So great was his trust in this comely OGPU agent that only the year before, when she had dined with him and his wife in Paris, he had frankly told her of his utter disgust with Stalin's bloody purges and cruelties, and of his despair at the internecine party conflicts.

She had sympathized with him deeply, adding: "I, also, think Stalin is making a grievous error."

From that remark, Reiss was sure he could trust her. It was September 3rd when he went to a Lausanne hotel where OGPU agents occasionally stayed, and inquired after the Schildbach woman. And, of course, the perfidious Gertrude was there! She had been ordered from Rome to Lausanne telegraphically by Speigelglass in Paris, on the chance that Reiss might succeed in beating his way into Switzerland, where they knew his wife resided.

To Gertrude, Reiss confided that he had severed relations with the OGPU as well as the Communist Party. She expressed approbation, and agreed once more that political events in Moscow were nauseous. For good measure, she accepted an invitation to dinner the next evening with Reiss.

The following afternoon the woman met Beletsky, the agent who had attended the Paris conference and who had rushed to Lausanne on Gertrude Schildbach's message that Reiss had bobbed up. Beletsky brought with him a box of poisoned candy, with instructions that the woman was to feed them to the agent who had incurred the wrath of Stalin in far-off Moscow. The candy, larded with strychnine, had been prepared by Beletsky, an expert toxicologist.

But this act of treachery was too much, even for Gertrude. Despite the agent's threats, she refused to be the direct instrument of Reiss' death. Beletsky, known as "The Doctor" to other agents, raved and threatened, and made it clear what would happen if she did not aid in the liquidation of Reiss.

At last, terrified, she consented to ask Reiss to take a walk that evening, after they had finished their dinner at an inn outside Lausanne. "Doctor" Beletsky now had to move fast.

Early on the evening of September 4th a quartet of men met on the outskirts of Lausanne. Besides the "doctor," there were two accomplices who had accompanied him from Paris; one Charles Martignat, known to OGPU colleagues as "The Red Assassin," and the other a man yet to be identified. The fourth member was Francois Rossi who had accompanied Gertrude Schildbach to Lausanne and was living in an adjoining room at the Hotel de la Paix.

It was Rossi who had obtained the hired car from the Steiner girl at Berne, and was to drive it on its murderous mission that evening. Martignat, judging from the blood-splattered condition in which the car was found, sat in the rear. Of the remaining two, one sat beside the driver, the other presumably sat next to "The Red Assassin."

A FEW minutes before, Reiss and his woman companion had finished their dinner. He told of his relief at escaping from France into Switzerland where, he thought, he was safe. It may be supposed that Gertrude wished him success in whatever sphere he built a new life with his patient, uncomplaining wife . . .

Though Gertrude Schildbach would not feed him strychnine, she was able to bring herself to propose a walk in the fading light, before they returned to Lausanne. Reiss agreed. It was a clear, cool night, and the snow on distant peaks, and the lake far below them, sparkled in the brilliant moonlight.

Behind them, Reiss heard the roar of a heavy car, climbing the grade. He grasped his companion's arm to move her to safety and, strangely, felt her trembling!

With a shrill scream of brakes, the heavy car stopped beside them.

Four men leaped from the machine.

Reiss was a muscular man, not easily frightened. He fought fiercely for several minutes but at last went down beneath the repeated blows of blackjacks.

The erstwhile OGPU agent was dragged into the heavy car. When it had gathered speed, with exhaust open, "The Red Assassin" lifted the light sub-machine-gun from the tonneau-floor where Reiss was lying, unconscious.

He "sprayed" Reiss from head to foot with the vicious, spitting weapon, as the police later deduced from the condition of the body and the fact that a number of bullet-holes were found in the floor of the machine.

Five hundred yards from the point where police found signs of a scuffle, the body was drawn from the car, to spill out its blood on the snow.

Thence the machine, whose occupants now included the Schildbach woman, raced away for Geneva and the midnight *rapide* for Paris.

There was no time to worry over the fate of that personable "tourist," Renata Steiner.

MARTIGNAT, who did the actual killing, escaped with Rossi to Mexico. Lydia Grozovskaya, who betrayed Reiss in Paris, was arrested there at the request of the Swiss police, but escaped from jail in boy's clothes, and is now reported working in Moscow. Gertrude Schildbach, the decoy, fearful of falling into the hands of the French or Swiss authorities, made her way to Moscow where, according to information in Paris, she has disappeared from sight. Her former associates are in no quandary over her fate, in view of her disinclination to simplify the assassination by feeding her friend strychnine. Renata Steiner still awaits trial as an accessory before the murder.

Inevitably, the Government of the Soviet Union denied any knowledge of the assassination. But in Paris the liquidation of Reiss provoked one of the agents of the Soviet secret service to remark sardonically, with a philosophical shrug of his shoulders:

"Well, you know, how the OGPU *discourages* the resignation of its men!"

CRIMINAL *laboratories can now examine from 400 to 500 fingerprints per minute through the use of newly constructed machines.*

THE DEVIL'S HANGWOMAN

By

Antoinette Chabert

A HOARSE shout of triumph, primeval and brutish, arose from the several hundred spectators. Furiously, the three judges of the Douai Court of Assizes rapped for order, while the police, scattered around the courtroom, made stern admonitions for quiet.

Such was the temper of the crowd that the cries and shouts increased in a crescendo of passion.

"Kill her now! Let us have her! She's too evil for the guillotine! We'll tear her apart and throw her to the dogs, the filthy pig!"

The faces of the crowd, con-

FRANCE: *Misguided mother-love, plus greed and jealousy make up the ingredients for one of the most cold-blooded murders in the annals of French crime.*

torted by hate and self-righteousness, suggested the time of the scene to be 1793, when infuriated Parisians spat at aristocrats passing down the Faubourg St. Honoré en route to the guillotine, yet, a calendar on the wall of the courtroom proclaimed it to be the year 1938.

Police quickly formed a cordon around the hysterical, weeping defendant, buxom 47-year-old Rosalie Mory. Beckoned from her bench, she fell to the floor in a faint and was carried away, unconscious, on an improvised stretcher.

The Mory case was something of a *cause celébré* even in France, which is not unaccumstomed to savage murders. It aroused the residents of the Douai region to a high pitch of anger because it was an unprecedented example of the lengths to which misguided mother-love, supplemented by thwarted pride and ambition, will go to seek revenge.

ROSALIE MORY had been married more than a quarter century to Louis Mory, who had a substantial textile business in Douai, once part of the war-devastated regions in north central France. They were not wealthy by American standards, but the couple were thrifty and by the time their only son, also named Louis, had attained his majority, the family was comfortably well-off.

Louis, as a youth, had shown considerable brilliance in school, and his parents—particularly his doting mother — expected great things of him, chief of which was an advantageous marriage. By this she meant, primarily, a marriage that would increase the Mory bank account.

Young Louis was, in his mother's view, one of the most attractive men in France. Possibly there was something not altogether normal in Mme. Mory's excessive fondness for her offspring. Because he was a lieutenant in the French Army Reserves and, for a stated number of weeks each year, could sport around Douai in his striking blue uniform, she fondly thought that every girl who saw him was instantly captivated.

"Say what you will," she would repeatedly tell neighbors and tradespeople, "there is no one like my Louis. One of these days the country will hear from him. And he'll make a brilliant marriage. I'll see to that! Mark my words."

Her listeners nodded their agreement. Mme. Mory, they said behind her back, was growing pretty tiresome about her marvelous Louis. She was a good woman, they agreed, but every year she grew more insufferable about her son. One would suppose, to listen to her, there was not another army officer in all France. And, after all, what was a lieutenant in the Reserves?

The Morys had worked hard

for their money, and moreover they lived in a part of modern Gaul that is noted for its uncanny ability to add every day to the gold reserve in the family sock. They believed they were doing an act of unparalleled parental sacrifice when they sent Louis to college. The youth rewarded their expenditure — which they could well afford — by obtaining outstanding marks in his studies.

But in Mme. Mory's eyes, that was far from sufficient. Louis must marry brilliantly, and the girl must have a dowry in keeping with his position, financially and socially.

"Don't marry" she told him, night and day, "unless I have found out all about the girl. And always take me into your confidence. Tell me everything, *mon petit.*"

To Rosalie Mory, Louis was still an infant in swaddling clothes although, in physical fact, he was six feet tall and well set-up, a typical specimen of the athletic, post-war Frenchman.

There is a strong tradition of filial obedience in France, and Louis consented to all the smothering exactments of his doting mother. But he had not counted on an experience he was to undergo last year in England. At this time, the lieutenant was twenty-four.

Despite their strong repugnance to spending money for other than necessaries, the Morys gave Louis funds for a short visit to England, which was an expedition designed to complete his formal schooling. The trip would give him an opportunity to try out his school English. He left Douai in high spirits.

From friends of his parents, he had obtained a letter of introduction to a Mr. and Mrs. Shepherd of Leeds. Louis went there to present it after a week spent in London. Staying with them at the time was an exquisite young French girl, Yvette Godefroy. She was a diminutive brunette who scarcely reached the lieutenant's elbow. In the case of Louis and Yvette, there was nothing fictional about love at first sight.

The girl had been an "exchange student" in a convent at Wakefield, where she had gone to perfect her English. She was soon to return to France. An orphan, she was going to serve as a governess to a family not distant from Douai. She had not a penny. To one whose life had been as cloistered as hers, Louis was the most glamorous individual she had ever encountered. Twenty-four hours after he met her, the young Frenchman impetuously proposed, and Yvette eagerly accepted him.

They returned to France together.

MLLE. GODEFROY had the usual nervousness of the fiancee over meeting her future in-laws. Despite Louis' assurances that his parents would be drawn to her not less than he was, the girl's fears were well-grounded. Half an hour after she had met Louis' mother, the fiancee was in tears and Rosalie Mory was screaming and howling in the Mory home, to the scandalous glee of the neighbors.

For Rosalie was furious. She had not been warned; she had not been advised. Her counsel had not been asked. How did Louis dare do anything so presumptuous! Their marriage was unthinkable. Hadn't the obscure girl said herself—trying pitifully to be gay and to ease the strained atmosphere—"I'm as poor as the proverbial church mouse, but honest."

"And I don't believe you're honest, either!" the mother had retorted.

Louis' father backed up his mother, although he was less vindicative. But the two men nearly came to blows. In the heat of the argument, Rosalie turned on her son and said:

"Your father and I have made every sacrifice to send you to college. You have repaid us by bringing this nobody into our home!"

Such charges and language were intolerable to the youth who had confidently expected an affectionate reception for his fiancee and himself at Douai. But his mother's fury and his father's disapproval of the girl in no way lessened his determination to marry her. They left the house together, and Louis found simple lodgings for her on the outskirts of the town. Then he returned to the family domicile to face his parents down.

"Who is this wretched girl?" his mother raged. "Who are her family. She has none! Can't you see that this Yvette, or whatever she calls herself, is an adventuress? She just wants the security of your name and our purse."

The son tried to reason with his mother who, he realized with a shock, was less disapproving of the girl than insanely jealous of her. He flung out of the house for a second time, after listening to an hour-long harangue, and told his parents quietly:

"I'm not coming back. Yvette and I will be married in a week. What difference does it make that she's an orphan? I love her. Perhaps afterward you'll both come to your senses."

Mme. Mory could not believe that her son would leave the family hearth. But when she saw him storm out, she had no intention of accepting defeat. She left in a few minutes and paid a visit to a private detective in Douai. She wanted evidence derogatory to Yvette and was not over particular in what manner it was gathered, or, for that matter, its authenticity. The private detective told her she had nothing to fear. In a few hours he would have all the information that madame desired.

The private detective established that Yvette had been reared in Rouen. From various sources he learned that she was "gay", which the investigator translated for his client to mean "loose", that she spent most of her time in disreputable cafes patronized by poilus and sailors, that she had been in trouble with police for a variety of petty offenses.

All these charges he substantiated with a collection of forged documents. Whether he admitted to Mme. Mory that they were forgeries was not disclosed, but in any event Louis' mother had what she desired. She lost no time in summoning her son, on the pretext that she wanted to effect a reconciliation.

Once she had her son cornered in her living-room, she showed him the "affidavits".

"You see, my son? The girl's demure, innocent manner is a fraud. Surely you recognize now that you cannot possibly marry her. If you will not think of yourself, consider the disgrace you will bring down on your poor father and myself. Dismiss her. Give her a few francs, and send her packing!"

Louis laughed in his mother's face, which made her jealousy all the greater.

"I don't believe those charges for an instant," he retorted. "I know Yvette so well that it's farcical to say she ever had an evil thought in her head."

Again he left.

Yvette protested that she did not want to come between his mother and himself. He must try to effect a genuine reconciliation. Otherwise neither Louis nor herself could be happy.

IT WAS not difficult for Yvette to tell Louis where to get evidence completely refuting the charges made in the detective's affidavits. The easily ascertainable truth was that Yvette had been cared for by an order of Catholic sisters in Rouen, where she went to the local *lycée*. Her marks were such that she won the exchange scholarship to the convent in Leeds.

She had never had any boyfriends, despite her almost spectacular beauty, because she had spent all her life in convents. She was entirely unworldly. Even had she craved them, the girl had had no opportunity for extramural adventures.

With this valid rebuttal, Louis returned to his home. He revealed to his mother that the detective had fabricated the evidence against Yvette. But Mme. Mory merely scoffed at her son's evidence of his fiancee's good repute. This time Louis made it definite that he would not return, even if his mother begged forgiveness on her knees.

Louis and Yvette married. He was without a penny and, of course, so was she. The haste of their marriage was partly due to the fact that the girl was going to have a child. The young couple were so deeply in love that they had not waited for a religious ceremony to bind their union.

Unknown to them, Mme. Mory discovered that fact, and it intensified her hatred of Yvette tenfold. Unquestionably, in her mind, the girl had trapped her incomparable son into lending his name to a child which, doubtless had been fathered by some drunken sailor or soldier.

The mother did not hesitate to spread the news. Her immaculate son had been snared by a designing orphan girl who was probably illegitimate. She had worked on his pity and forced him to marry her. But, surprising to Mme. Mory, her malicious gossip was received with repugnance. A few neighbors had the temerity to stand up and reproach her for her cruelty to the girl.

Even if one half she charged were true, neighbors said, her magnificent son had married the girl. Common decency and maternal loyalty demanded that Mme. Mory help the young couple make a success of their lives. Louis had to marry some one, didn't he? And certainly Yvette looked and acted as a quiet, respectable young woman.

Mme. Mory had boasted so long of her son's virtues that it was inevitable that a good many of her acquaintances secretly were glad she was having difficulties with him. But, apart from that human reaction, the community feeling against her was strong because of her indifference to the fact that her daughter-in-law would soon have a child. They could not understand her callousness in the face of motherhood.

One consequence of the feeling against the older woman was that her husband's business began to fall off. Many Douai residents decided they would buy their textiles elsewhere. As in the case of most French families, the exchequer is the wife's concern, and Mme. Mory was quick to note the slackening of income.

Already burning with hatred for Yvette because the girl had enmeshed her model son, the sudden assault on her pocket-book made that hate, if possible, still deeper. She saw her son abandoned to vice, and her husband and herself reduced to beggary, as the result of the machinations of Yvette Godefroy Mory.

Why had she ever permitted the boy to go to England! What might now be done to end a situation fraught with ruin?

WHILE Rosalie Mory was considering means of alienating Louis from Yvette, the young married couple were having a difficult time making ends meet. Without money from his parents, the son had been forced to move his bride into a cottage that was scarcely more than a hovel. He had work as a clerk but the pay was insufficient to feed and clothe them, and to pay rent. The entire town knew of their difficulties and friends were sympathetic. For the elder Morys were one of the wealthiest families in Douai.

About two months before the child was expected to be born, Mme. Mory again appeared on the scene. She appeared repentent and eager for a reconciliation. At first, Yvette received her warmly. She did not want any of the Morys' money, she told her husband; she would prefer that they make their way alone, however hard it might be at first. She had so much confidence in him. But she felt that his life would be less desperate if he could make his peace with his mother.

Louis refused his mother's offers of aid. But he was affectionate to her. Her visits to the wretched home became more frequent, and she insisted on helping Yvette in the kitchen, arguing that the girl needed plenty of rest before her confinement.

One night, in a fit of nerves, the bride confessed to her husband she feared to have her mother-in-law do anything in the preparation of food.

"Yvette, you're being silly!" Louis protested. "Why, Mother may be difficult but—she's not a murderess! *Mon Dieu!* Don't be a child!"

But as the days progressed, Louis could see that his mother was becoming increasingly domineering. She ordered Yvette around as though the young wife were no more than a slave. Nervous because of the approaching childbirth, Yvette was made even more distraught by her mother-in-law's criticism, by her veiled insinuations that there was something suspicious in the girl's background.

Ironically, as Yvette's despair increased, Louis believed that his mother was becoming more tractable. He sought to calm his wife's vague fears and premonitions and, privately, attributed them to a condition of nerves that was only normal in any woman expecting a child.

One night he told her, after she brought herself to beg that he keep Mme. Mory from their home:

"But you've urged me all along to try and compromise with her. I know she's difficult, but I have felt she was really growing to like you."

"Yes! Yes! That's why I'm afraid of her! Don't you see?"

"But what are you frightened about? She's not a monster!"

"I don't know what I'm afraid of—that's what terrifies me!"

"Please, Yvette," he pleaded, "try to tolerate her for a while longer. She and Father can be very helpful to us. When she recognizes that she can't come between us, she'll be sensible once again. Believe what I say, she's not a monster!"

But, later, Louis several times had to order his mother from the house. One such ejection occurred after she said to him at dinner, in front of Yvette, "How do you know it's your child?" But the next day she would re-appear at the cottage, full of contrition and apologies, and force her way indoors.

JUST as animals are said to smell fear, and to take advantage of it, so Mme. Mory knew the girl was in mortal dread of her. But none of this was evident to her son, and he continued to minimize his wife's confessions of terror.

But last Autumn, the Mory woman reached a point where she could no longer control her fury. Yvette's baby was expected in a fortnight. The girl moved with difficulty. When the mother-in-law appeared at the cottage, soon after Louis had left for work, Yvette was unable to bar her entrance.

Once inside the kitchen, she offered the girl a bag in which, she said, were some sweet buns. As the weak Yvette reached out a hand, the mother-in-law seized her by the throat.

With her strong fingers, she strangled the girl, gripping her throat till the once-lovely eyes protruded and the face grew blue.

Then, contemptuously she thrust Yvette from her, letting the body drop to the floor when it no longer showed signs of life. Because Yvette was soon to give birth to a child, Mme. Mory had actually committed two murders.

Mme. Mory next undid the paper bag which was supposed to contain buns. From it she drew a strong clothes-line.

The line had been made into a noose. Tightly she drew it around the girl's neck, and pulled the other end taut over a hook on the back of the front door. Near the girl's feet she overturned a chair.

Mme. Mory believed that she had made it appear that Yvette had taken her own life. The police, she reasoned, would conclude that Yvette had stepped on the chair, fastened the noose around her neck, the other end to the hook, then kicked it from under her.

Foolishly, Mme. Mory thought that the finger-marks around the girl's throat would be attributed to the bruises caused by the clothes-line.

Less than an hour after the hysterical young husband, almost insane with grief, had found his wife's body, his mother was under arrest. At the trial, the defendant laughed and wept in turn. She thought to extenuate herself on grounds that the girl had ruined her son's career.

When her husband was called to the stand, he told of how he had gone to Yvette and tried to induce her not to go through with the marriage.

"But then she told me that she would soon be a mother," he said, anger suffusing his face, "and so

I told her she could raise the brat herself."

Spectators shouted their fury at this brutal admission. The judges ordered the courtroom cleared for the duration of that day.

The highlight of the trial was the tongue-lashing to which the defendant was subjected by the prosecutor. It was one of the most venomous summaries in the history of murder trials in France, and was avidly read and approved in every corner of the nation.

The prosecutor gave her no mercy. It so affected Mme. Mory that, at intervals, she burst into loud sobs, beat her breast, and screamed for him to desist. Throughout, the trial was constantly interrupted by the irrepressible jeers of the spectators.

THE THREE judges of the Douai Court of Assizes strode impressively to their seats. Over the courtroom, packed with restive spectators and watchful gendarmerie, there fell an expectant hush.

The jurist in the center rapped his gavel smartly.

"There will be no commotion, *messieurs, mesdames,*" he warned.

Then turning to the defendant in the prisoner's box, he proclaimed:

"Rosalie Josephine Mory, the judges of this court find you guilty of the murder of your daughter-in-law. For this terrible crime you will die beneath the knife of the guillotine!"

Under the French custom, she was not told when she would die. She will not know until five minutes before the time of her execution. When that time comes, a guard will bring her the pint of brandy which the French Republic gives those it executes.

And now, Mme. Mory, from hour to hour, awaits commutation of the death sentence from President Lebrun—or the arrival of the priest, her lawyer, and a guard with a flask of brandy in his pocket.

ON June 8th, 1936, Michael Milligan, a poet of San Francisco, shot and killed Mrs. Camilla Smith, because he was jealous of the attentions paid his estranged wife by Mrs. Smith. Milligan fled into a wild and desolate region where the police and a volunteer posse searched for him in vain. Fourteen months later, on August 26th, 1937, a Pioche, Nevada, policeman with a photographic memory, picked up a man whose face he had seen on a wanted circular more than a year before. It was Milligan. The killer was returned to California so that justice may take its proper course.

AT THE SIGN OF THE ANGEL

By
Wilfred Fang Chao

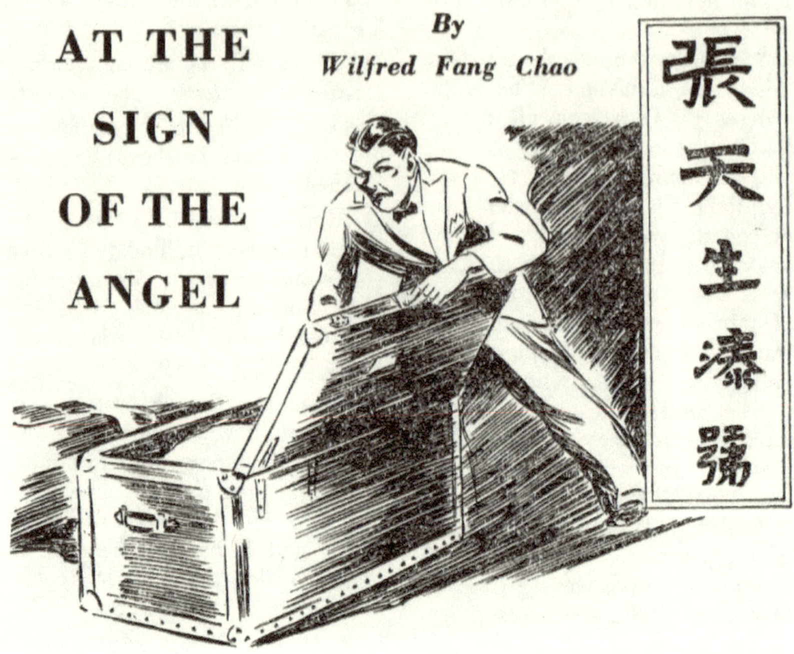

KNOTS of welcomers limply shuffled, waiting, at the Kobe pier as the *Shanghai Maru,* bound for Yokahama, from Shanghai, maneuvered to its berth. Up went the gangplank and down slid the Kobe passengers, fanning and mopping themselves. For the heat, on this mid-afternoon of August 7th, was gruelling. In ones and twos the passengers filtered through the Customs barrier with their luggage. Friends and kinsmen detached themselves from the waiting clusters, and within an hour the pier had all but lost life and interest.

The officers of the Japanese Imperial Customs, glad of another day well done and over, prepared to leave. Waterfront laborers were making things shipshape when—

JAPAN: *A mysterious trunk, discharged at the wrong port, sets in motion the resources of the efficient Japanese police; and a silent traveler begins a journey that was to bring a murderous lover to justice.*

"*Ara!* What's this!" exclaimed a junior customs man.

"What's what?" a colleague demanded.

"This baggage!" pointed its discoverer. The "baggage" was a new-looking, compact trunk. The two strode over to examine it. They had no need to get very near to catch the sticky, acrid odor it exuded.

"Whew!" the second customs man protested. "What the devil's in it?"

They examined the label attentively. It showed the trunk to be the property of Mr. Q. H. Man, traveling first-class to Yokahama.

"A fine business!" said one, exasperated. "There'll be the devil to pay over such a stupid blunder, discharging the trunk at the wrong port!"

"It's no affair of ours," remarked the other, placidly. "We can only report it."

The report was duly made, setting in motion a train of numerous consultations and telephone discussions. The operators of the steamship line were unable to find a Mr. Q. H. Man on the passenger list of the *Shanghai Maru.* Officials of the company and of the Customs had a further look at the trunk. They could make even less of it now than before. Its odor had thickened progressively along with its mysteriousness.

They considered this latter feature now. Without straining a fair-minded man's credulity, they believed that the trunk's objectionable aroma could be made the company's excuse for having put the piece of luggage off the boat. That would save everybody's face which: led to the question uppermost in all minds—what foul smell was Mr. Q. H. Man introducing around Asia!

After some debate they decided upon an even further step; to make an official inspection of the contents. The trunk was opened and, as they peered into it, the senior inspector promptly slammed down the lid, and stepped back in horror. For in the trunk was a body in a badly decomposed condition.

"Summon the police!" commanded the official. He made out a report of the proceedings up to this point, and those who had witnessed the finding of the body stepped up and signed below the officer's signature.

"*Sa!*" snorted a subordinate. "Instead of going home we will have to stand by for a million questions the police will ask."

UNFORTUNATELY for the witnesses, who urgently longed to get a good cleansing bath, the police took a much more serious view of the matter than anyone had foreseen. To the Kobe police—and they are among the most efficient in the world—the case had a strictly local angle. Investigation would have to be made of the strange circumstances surrounding the discharging of the trunk at the wrong port. For, as to that, the body could have been planted on the pier, to throw the police off the trail.

The individual witnesses were cross-questioned thoroughly, and their names taken for further examination. It was well into the night before they were permitted to go and bathe in something more refreshing than their own sweat.

Meanwhile, the police realized that there was an admissable possibility of an international angle to the affair. If this proved so, the national authorities no doubt would wish to intervene. They safeguarded themselves on this point by wiring all known details to Tokyo and to the Japanese Consular Police at Shanghai.

The body was definitely within the Kobe jurisdiction and, until it could be proved to be the remains of, say, a confidential employee of the Imperial Service, or the victim of international anti-Japanese intrigue, it was the view of the local police that it was their responsibility.

The next step was to identify the victim. The body was that of a woman, garbed in Chinese clothes; though, for that matter, this proved nothing. The texture of the hair did indicate her to be an Oriental, however. Due to the condition of the body nothing more than these few facts could be determined.

At the morgue, the cause and time of her death were quickly fixed. She had been killed by blows on the head with a blunt instrument, some five days or a week prior to the discovery of her body.

This set the date at around August 1st. It remained, as yet, to verify the statement of the Customs that the trunk must have been discharged from the *Shanghai Maru*. By radioed request of Kobe authorities, officers of the boat, now approaching Yokahama, questioned the crew about the trunk. A steward was found who swore that it was put aboard at Shanghai.

This took the matter out of the Kobe police jurisdiction, and they accordingly advised the Japanese Consular Police at Shanghai. Arrangements were promptly made, too, to ship the trunk and its grisly contents back to the Chinese metropolis on the *Nagasaki Maru*.

For, without the corpus delicti, the Shanghai authorities could not, of course, prove that the crime had been committed, if or when they should find the murderer.

In Shanghai, the first cabled police report from Kobe caused an instant stir. Local resentment against Japan at that time was daily mounting. This feeling showed itself, wherever it dared, in sporadic outbursts against individual Japanese subjects. The body shipped from Shanghai to Kobe could be the first victim of a deliberate campaign of terror.

It was vital that the scheme, if

such it were, be smashed with swift and heavy hand.

THE JAPANESE force at Shanghai had two strikes on it before it could even begin, however. In the first place, at that stage of the case, what Kobe had been able to cable was not much to go on in tracking down a supposed crime. The corpse of an Oriental female had been found in a trunk in Kobe—now to find the murderer in Shanghai's slinking labyrinths.

In the second place, police processes in Shanghai, as in other treaty ports of China, were complex. In addition to Japan's Consular Police there, the French and International Settlement each had its independent police force, while the Chinese had jurisdiction outside the international foreign quarters.

A further complication was the jealously guarded extraterritorial right of each Consulate to try cases involving its own nationals. The victim was an Oriental: England, Holland, Portugal, France and even the United States, have Asiatic nationals.

There was only one thing for the Japanese corps to do, and this they did at once. They informed their colleagues at the various "Settlements," of the known circumstances of the case and then set out to do their own best.

The first point of attack was, of course, the pier. Police circulated about, putting questions here and there. But no one on the wharf had noticed any particular trunk. There are so many trunks on steamer-day!

"Very well!" growled the chief of the police detail. "Let's seek elsewhere!"

"There was only one trunk," a subordinate reminded. "Could it not have been brought by 'riksha?"

"Of course! And you think other 'riksha men would have noticed that? So do I!"

They got busy in that direction and their reasoning and efforts bore fruit. Two men in the jinriksha line-up recalled the trunk and its owner.

"I remember it!" exclaimed one of the 'riksha men. "There were two jinriksha: one with a heavy trunk, one with a small man. My friend, Chung, noticed the man because he looked like a half-caste. I think he was a Japanese, myself."

"Why?"

"His trunk was bright and new."

"And what of it? What has that to do with it?"

"Japanese like to be conspicuous," retorted the Chinese coolie saucily.

"Hold your tongue, you!" snapped the police officer.

But with that much information, the police were still far from an arrest. However it was all progress in the right direction. They questioned the baggage-master at the entrance to the pier.

"An Eurasian with one new trunk, for the *Shanghai Maru?*" this functionary reflected. "Yes—I think I recall such a circumstance. Yes; now I remember. He came in a jinriksha, with his trunk in another behind him. An unwholesome looking sort of fellow."

"That is very probably our man," judged the police chief. "So he was really a half-caste then?"

"Why—er," hesitated the baggage-master. "That, or else Japanese—he spoke no Chinese except Shanghai dialect, and that very brokenly."

"So!" the chief exclaimed. "How can we find him, I wonder?"

"I shall call the man who carried the trunk aboard," said the baggage-master. He raised his voice, peremptorily summoning a coolie by name. The call was taken up along the wharf; and shortly, up pattered a laborer.

"Tell these officers all you can remember," scowled the functionary impressively, "about that Eurasian whose shiny new trunk you carried onto the *Shanghai Maru* on the last trip out."

"Well," grunted the man. "He was not Chinese, I can tell you. Eurasian, as my master says. I set down his trunk where he ordered, and that is all I know."

"Did you not see the 'rikshaman who brought the trunk to the wharf?"

"I suppose so."

"You do not know him, though? You did not speak?"

"No; I was busy that day. The Eurasian was too impatient to get his precious trunk aboard."

The police were left groping once more.

THEN aid cam from an unexpected quarter. An inkling of the weird case got out to some of the local Chinese newspaper editors and they sent reporters after the particulars.

"We have the matter well in hand," said the Consular Police Chief stonily. The reporters could not get any more out of him. For, in fact, at that moment there was nothing he could tell them. The representatives of the press gave up. They were on the point of leaving, when, in came the police wharf-detail to report its findings.

Standing aside as inconspicuously as possible, the reporters got the story before the Chief of Police could hush up his men. In that evening's papers the story appeared in as much detail as it had been uncovered thus far.

The Japanese Consular authorities were disgusted at this meddlesome publicity given the case at so delicate a stage. But they soon changed their minds about that, when an official of the International Settlement Police telephoned.

"A detective attached to the Chinese police is here at the station," he said. "He read about the Kobe trunk-murder case in this evening's paper."

"An unfortunate case all around," returned the Japanese officer icily.

"He thinks he has a lead you may wish to follow up," came the other's voice.

"Eh?" the Japanese listened sharply.

"Yes. He tells us he saw a short-statured Eurasian angrily quarreling with a Chinese girl on August 3rd, outside Number 13, Kashing Road."

"Kashing Road Number 13," jotted down the officer. "It may lead us to something tangible, at least. Many thanks to you!"

Within the hour, the vicinity of 13 Kashing Road swarmed with sleuths dispatched by the Japanese Consular Police. That neighborhood was within the International Settlement, and the Japanese police had no authority in that quarter, though enjoying the courtesy-right of unofficially operating detectives there in the pursuit of the case at hand. However, interrogations or arrests, if any, could be rightfully made only by the International Settlement force.

Next door to No. 13, a Madam Chang operated a rooming-house over her son's store. The large signs, displayed to attract attention, did not escape the speculative notice of the detectives. This establishment's existence was reported, along with other observations of vaguely possible significance.

Two roving detectives of rank were sent to the neighborhood.

"Madam Chang's rooming-house interests me, somehow," said the senior detective as they approached the place along the opposite side of the street, the better to size it up.

"*T'ien shêng t'ai yung*: At the Sign of the Angel," translated the matter-of-fact junior of the pair, reading the huge signs hanging, horizontal and perpendicular, before Madam Chang's establishment. "Are you going in?"

His colleague was already half way across the street.

MADAM CHANG appeared grudgingly. She had seen them coming and was patently under no illusion as to the Japanese men's business.

"Well!" she demanded abruptly. "What is it?"

"A Eurasian man was noticed fighting with a Chinese girl outside your door on August 3rd. Possibly this may have a bearing on a murder committed a day or two later. We want to know whatever you can tell us of the Eurasian or his lady friend."

"I know nothing!" said the old lady emphatically. "I am not required to tell you what I know!"

"You know something, though, eh?" seized the detective quickly.

"Admit nothing," growled her son, appearing suddenly, scowling blackly at the two Nipponese. "Go

—go! Ask your prying questions elsewhere!"

This was all the two plainclothesmen needed. By arrangement, the International Settlement force stepped in. There was no evading these officers, and the Changs knew it. Madam Chang quaked with alarm at the threatening course the affair was taking.

"A half-caste man took lodgings in my house," she whined, prepared to tell as much as she knew. "He came with a young female. It was towards the end of July—the 26th," she added at the command to be specific.

"How long did he stop at your place?"

"They left four or five days ago —I—I mean on the fifth day of the present month," stammered Madam Chang.

" 'They' left — together? You saw them, yourself, leaving together on August 5th?" quickly demanded the police officer.

"Well—I"—she hesitated.

"Think well!" he sharply counselled, seeing in her eye a half-intention to utter a falsehood.

"No."

"When did you last see the woman then—before or after the man left?"

"The night before," the old lady grumbled.

"Interesting," the policeman pointed out to confreres flanking him. "Tell us everything," he added to Madam Chang. "Everything you noticed about this Eurasian."

"Their quarrels were their private affair!" Madam Chang raised her voice as she regained her old self-assurance.

"Their quarrels? Come! Come! Start at the beginning and tell us the whole story!" His frigid authority intimidated her anew. She obeyed almost meekly.

The little Eurasian and his lady-friend came seeking a room. They were plainly queer, but seemed respectable enough people, such as they were: he paid cash on account and promised more. She could not help noticing how he unmercifully scorched the Shanghai dialect, and that his companion had a horribly Cantonese accent; but, as Madam Chang was ready to admit from her seasoned observation, "we cannot all be fortunate."

"What name did he give?" interrupted one of the police agents.

"What name? Why, he gave no name. What business would that be of mine?"

The policeman shrugged ruefully. It would have been an alias, in any case, he mused.

"His name!" sniffed the proprietress again impatiently, and resumed her account—

THE man and his sweetheart installed themselves in a room that evening, with their belongings. Their bickering started almost at once and—Madam Chang had not believed her ears at first—

by midnight the pair had passed from words to blows. Going discreetly to investigate the muffled noise, she heard everything. It sounded, she said, as though he slapped the girl, not once but three or four times, each blow evoking exasperated abuse from her.

The disturbances went on day after day and the fights seemed to become more bitter. Each night there was bedlam At the Sign of the Angel. The other lodgers complained; the proprietress was distraught.

Yet the pair were not always at war. They would issue out in the morning as happily as anyone could wish. That was the strange thing about them.

But on the night of August 3rd the fisticuffs and recriminations of the lovers had the whole house in an uproar.

Madam Chang banged on their door and ordered them to cease the disturbance at once and, furthermore, to have their things ready to leave in the morning. Speaking through his closed door, the half-caste apologized and so humbly begged another chance that Madam Chang consented to let them stay providing they behaved. And not a peep came out of that room the rest of the night.

The next morning the two went out, smiling, as nonchalant as children. They were in the same pleasant mood when they returned to The Angel that evening. Later, they went out again; evidently to a gay party, judging by their attire, and got back around midnight.

Then all at once inferno broke out with a fury. Their door was no sooner closed than from behind it came blows and fierce arguing. Suddenly one of them burst into shrill screams, not of anger but of terror.

"That was enough," concluded Madam Chang. "I went to their door right away and ordered them out of my house. 'Get out at once! Immediately!' I said. He came to the door and promised that there positively would be no further disturbance. I wanted them to go promptly; but at last let them stay —on condition that they leave the next morning without fail!"

"And that next morning was when you saw him leave—but you never saw her again?" questioned the officer.

Madam Chang nodded. "He told me that she had left at dawn. He went out and came back with a trunk. It was new. An Eurasian-looking friend was with him."

"How do you know he was a friend?"

"Oh, he had been in my house once or twice before, with my troublesome lodger," said Madam Chang.

The police seized this new information avidly. But up to this point, examine Madam Chang's story as they might, they were unable to get any particularly helpful lead as to the possible whereabouts of the Eurasian they were after.

"What language did the Eurasian speak to his friend?"

"Foreign," said the proprietress, adding at their insistence: "It was not Chinese, not even bad Chinese: it was foreign — how should I know what dialect of the Foreign language it was?"

This was all they could learn.

MEANWHILE, Japanese detectives were making a more careful survey of the immediate neighborhood. They discovered that a Portuguese employee of the Municipal Fire Department lived directly across the street from the room their Eurasian quarry had occupied. They reported this to their colleagues of the International Settlement.

On August 9th, obedient to a summons of the police, this employee, named DaSilva, appeared for examination at the Police Office. Questioned closely, he frankly answered them.

The Eurasian who had occupied the room At the Sign of the Angel was known to DaSilva—in fact they had been acquainted for some years. The name of the man they sought was Patricio Remedios. His father had been Portuguese and his mother Japanese.

"I thought I glimpsed them as they were rampaging in their room on the night before Patricio went away—and I think he struck her twice with a shoe or some object, perhaps," said DaSilva.

"Have you any idea what the matter was between the two of them?"

"Well," responded DaSilva somewhat hesitatingly. "According to general gossip: it is commonly believed that Patricio's affairs with women runs beyond the normal bounds. I have known a few of these woman and they have spoken to me of Patricio's brutality: his evident satisfaction in beating them."

"Did they ever tell you, in these confidences, why they stood for it?"

DaSilva shook his head, puzzled. "No. Perhaps they associated with him without knowing what to expect: most of them broke off with him as soon as they could, when they found out. But with Marie Tjin, it seemed to be a matter of liking it; or being so enamored of Patricio that she accepted her beatings from loyalty."

"Marie Tjin is—?"

"The woman he had with him At the Sign of the Angel!" said DaSilva.

At birth her parents, who were too poor to be able to keep a daughter, sold her into slavery to a Chinese woman who had the purchase price of three Chinese dollars and the patience to wait for the infant to attain the working age of four years.

Marie served this woman for twelve years, faithfully ministering and thereby getting a serviceable education at the same time. Her mistress was in frequent association with foreigners, and Marie had her introduction to those people and their languages at a tender age.

But then the elder woman did an incredible thing. She married one of the barbarians! As might have been expected he had prejudices about numerous things of which he had no understanding, and amongst these was the keeping of slaves. It seemed that Americans (he was an American sailor) felt very, very strongly on this particular idiosyncracy; and Marie found herself thrust out to shift for herself.

In this she was successful, to a certain extent. Finally Marie became enamored of an American sailor of her own. They were quite content with each other, and would not have severed their relations, had not the sailor introduced Marie to a friend. The friend was Patricio Remedios.

THE POLICE obtained photographs of Patricio and Marie and showed them to Madam Chang, who recognized them as her late lodgers. Patricio's widowed mother was discovered living in Shanghai. When the police entered her room, they found Remedios calmly eating his breakfast.

But Patricio refused to surrender. He was Portuguese by citizenship and he knew that he could not be arrested without a warrant from the Portuguese Consul at Shanghai. The Consul could not issue such a warrant under his nation's law, except upon proof that a crime had been committed.

And there was no proof, yet!

The Japanese Consular Police, however, had received word from the Kobe authorities that they were sending proof—the corpse of Marie Tjin—on the *Nagasaki Maru*. But the *Nagasaki Maru* would not arrive until August 13th—three days away!

While the witness was on the high seas—a silent traveler returning home to bring her demoniac sweetheart to justice—the police kept the Remedios house surrounded night and day, never losing sight or track of the Eurasian for an instant.

At last, on August 14th, they got the necessary warrant of seizure and detention from the Portuguese Consul, and Patricio was whisked off.

Searching the Remedios home, detectives found a blotter on which was indelibly mirrored the name on the trunk-label: Mr. Q. H. Man!

That clinched the case.

Patricio was extradited, under international law, to the Portuguese settlement at Macao, historic trading port in the south of China There he was quickly tried and sentenced to spend the rest of his days at hard labor on the island of Timor—a hellishly hot dot in the Malay Archipelago: a Portuguese Devil's Island.

BRIDE OF DEATH

By

Michael Jurbala

IMPATIENTLY waiting outside the apartment, the police heard someone softly playing Schumann's *Traumerei* on the piano. It was 10:30 at night as the liquid notes kept rising and falling, the pianist unheedful of the persistent rapping of the officers at the door.

"Break it down!" the commandant ordered gruffly, irked at the lack of response.

Three of the burly Czech officers hurled themselves against the frail portal. It gave way with a splintering crash, the men falling headlong into a foyer. Before they could regain their balance, th music stopped abruptly . . . ther was the stacato note of a pisto shot and the dull thud of a fallin body.

The police rushed into the hal beyond and stumbled over a man groaning and writhing in agon on the living-room floor. Ther was an ugly wound just above th right eye: in his right hand h held a revolver in a vise-like grip Nearby stood an expensive concert-grand, the overturned pian stool resting across the man's feet

The police commandant of th city of Brno ordered the ma

CZECHOSLOVAKIA: *A simple request for a pencil brings death to a highly respected Judge of the Circuit Court and a long jail sentence to a demure and beautiful girl.*

---

rushed to the nearest hospital. Then he led a search of the expensively furnished apartment of the highly respected Circuit Court Judge Jan Velgo.

Suddenly, from the bathroom, one of the offices let out a horrified shout.

"Good God! Look here!—the judge! Murdered!"

In answer to the alarm, the others stared, pop-eyed, at the body of the jurist, submerged in the tub. The water was crimson from blood that had flowed from a deep gash in the dead man's head.

"He's been dead about 15 minutes," the medical examiner pronounced, a few moments after his arrival. "The cause almost certainly was drowning. The other man may live. There's no doubt he attempted suicide."

THE COMMANDANT, certain the jurist had been murdered, began a methodical search of the apartment for clues. Unlocking the door of a closet in one of the bedrooms, he was startled to find a young woman slumped, unconscious, on the floor.

The officer carried her onto a chaise-lounge and began to rub her hands. He judged her to be about 20 and extremely pretty. She had the luxuriant blue-black hair characteristic of Slavic women, attractive petite features and a seductive figure.

It was not long before she opened her eyes with a flicker and began to whimper: "My husband! Where is my beloved husband? What has happened?"

"Who is your husband?" the commandant asked.

"Judge Velgo—where is he?"

The officer showed his skepticism. He knew Judge Velgo well: a man of considerable political influence and some degree of wealth. Slightly eccentric perhaps, and if gossip could be believed, rather esoteric in his tastes.

But what was certain was that the murdered jurist was a bachelor. Yet, here was an alluring young woman, many years his junior, calling Judge Velgo her husband! Surely there was trouble enough without this added nonsense.

The officer told her what had happened without mincing words, reasoning that a brutal explanation might shock the girl into telling the truth. But instead of provoking her to talk, her reaction to the bald account of the murder and attempted suicide was to fall into a dead faint.

When she had been revived a second time, she identified herself as Marie Havlick Velgo, her age as 21. Six weeks ago, she said, she had married the well-known jurist and sportsman on his fifty-fifth birthday. To the doubting police, she exhibited her marriage contract and wedding certificate.

A phone call was sufficient to convince the police the girl was telling the truth. Yet it was strange that Judge Velgo had not announced his nuptials. And even more incredible, the commandant realized, that, in so small a city as Brno, where the jurist enjoyed considerable popularity and was known to hundreds of citizens, he could have kept the marriage a secret.

"We'll discuss your marriage afterward," he told the pretty widow, as he held a vial of smelling salts beneath the tiny, retrousse nose. "Tell us first, all you know about this business."

"I recall very little," the young woman said, averting her eyes as police passed through the room bearing the judge's body on a stretcher to the morgue wagon. "My husband kept a professional engagement this evening, and I decided to retire early—get into bed and read a novel."

"Did you actually get into bed, and at what time?"

"No. The judge left about 8:30, saying he would return at 10 o'clock. I remember that I passed through the bedroom into the drawing-room to get the novel."

"Then—?"

"Then someone seized me from behind, placed a hand over my mouth, dragged me back into the bedroom and tossed me into the closet. I must have fainted from fear or lack of air. That's all I can remember, Commandant."

She could not—or would not—describe her assailant. Thus the police deemed it futile to take her to the hospital to look at the man found on the floor near the piano.

THE YOUNG woman's story could be true, the police conceded. Attempting to reconstruct the crime, they recognized that a burglar might have made his way into the jurist's apartment with a pass-key, believing no one to be home. When he found the young wife there, he seized her, threw her into the closet, and locked it.

Conceivably, when about to search for valuables, he heard the foyer door open. The robber could have ambushed Judge Velgo, struck him down with a jimmy or other tool, and, losing his head, have dragged him to the bathroom, filled the tub and held him under water.

The commotion in the apartment had been heard by Ottoker Zamarazil, the chief of the Czechoslovakian Press Bureau in Brno, who occupied the apartment below that of Judge Velgo. It was he who had summoned the police.

Yet, upon further examination, the burglar hypothesis would not hold water. It did not account for the piano-playing before police burst into the flat. But could the strains of *Traumerei* have come from another apartment? Quickly, the police established that the only piano in the building was in Judge Velgo's apartment.

Furthermore, a robber—assuming the judge's murderer was the man found on the drawing-room floor—would scarcely commit suicide, even when faced with capture. And finally, it was sheer fantasy to suppose that a burglar would play the piano after drowning the man whose home he planned to rob.

If robbery could be eliminated as a motive, what about the venerable triangle situation?

This seemed a more likely supposition. One of the detectives addressed the Commandant:

"Sir perhaps the situation was this:

"The Judge's young wife was in love with the man we found on the floor. The Judge returned earlier than expected, and found them in an embrace—remember she was in a negligee.

"Judge Velgo attacked the younger man, or vice versa. The man struck him, possibly with this milk bottle I found near the piano. He hauled him into the bathroom and drowned him while the judge was still unconscious, for there are no signs of a struggle there.

"Then, in an agony of remorse over the slaying, the two lovers decided to die together. But he hadn't the heart to shoot her. Instead, he picked her up, placed her in the small, airless closet, and locked the door, expecting her to die of suffocation.

"Then he sat down to the piano. You recall what he was playing? *Traumerei*—his sentimental farewell to an unrealistic dream. When he heard us at the door, he shot himself."

While the Commandant was considering this angle, the phone rang. He answered it, talked for half a minute, then carefully, slowly cradled the receiver.

"That's an ingenious theory, Lieutenant," he said, turning to the detective, "but I'm afraid it won't stand up. I was just talking to Headquarters. They have identified the man at the hospital as Wenzel Cerny. You remember him?"

The detective stared at his chief in surprise.

Cerny and the police of Brno had an acquaintance that began about a decade before. He had been in jail for petty larceny, arson, assault-and-robbery, and fraud. He was not a big-time crook, but one of hundreds of petty criminals chronically unable to keep out of jail.

The authorities, accordingly, were forced to admit that the case was not as simple as it had first appeared. They would have to dig into the background of Judge Velgo, Marie Havlick and Wenzel Cerny. In that way they might run across the key to the mystery.

POLICE officials had thought themselves well acquainted with Judge Velgo, since he had charge of the criminal section of the Circuit Court. Members of the Brno force frequently appeared before him as witnesses for the State. They knew that he was devoted to sports, particularly to skiing, hiking and running, despite the fact that he suffered from spinal curvature.

They had also heard that he was eccentric in some ways, and there had been rumors that he was "psychologically abnormal." This no one took seriously; such whispered charges are often made against men in prominent positions, or against individuals whose popularity is envied. It had also been bruited about the community that he was parsimonious, but that also was deprecated in view of the jurist's large circle of friends whom he entertained at many functions of all sorts.

Yet, the rumors that he was "psychologically abnormal" might bear investigation, the commandant mused, especially in a case that refused to fall into the convential categories of murder. The official decided to inquire into the personal life of the dead man, and meanwhile he booked the infuriated Marie Havlick Velgo as a material witness.

Cerny, the doctors said, might be sufficiently recovered to talk in three days.

The first move was to search the apartment thoroughly.

A peculiarity they soon noted was the preponderance of paintings of nudes. This fixation of the jurist was further reflected in his library, which overflowed with volumes of *erotica.* All the *erotica* permitted by law was there, as well as other volumes on such phenomena. This seemed incongruous in the home of one of the most eminent propounders of the law in Czechoslavakia. Scattered in corners and niches of the apartment were various exotic statues.

"Evidently Judge Velgo's interests extended far beyond the dusty tomes of the law," observed the commandant, musingly.

In the locked compartment of the judge's desk, police found receipts for payments of scores of "personals" in the classified columns of newspapers. The jurist, moreover, had kept copies of these peculiar insertions in the Czech press. One such "personal," typical of many others, read as follows:

> MONEY TO LEND — Philanthropist will extend small loans, without interest or security, to young girls deserving of his disinterested aid. Address Box—

To judge by the correspondence in his desk and safe, and by such odd momentoes in his dresser drawers as coquetish garters, stockings, gloves and handkerchiefs, the jurist was far from "disinterested" in the "deserving young girls."

Other leads in the apartment disclosed that in 1920 Judge Velgo while living in Techsen, had narrowly escaped prosecution for seduction.

The investigators next devoted their efforts to learning something of Marie Havlick who, meantime, was vehemently protesting her innocence from a cell in the Brno Penetentiary for Women. They unearthed some significant morsels of information.

THE DAUGHTER of an apartment house janitor and his wife, Marie had blossomed into an extraordinary beauty by the time she was 16. She despised the class from which she came, and was determined to lift herself to a higher social plane. A perceptive, precocious girl, she recognized that her most effective weapon was her fragile, Dresden-doll beauty.

One of her earliest accomplishments was the mastering of German, which widened her circle of acquaintances, hitherto restricted to Czechs. That achievement cost her parents nothing, Marie paying for the schooling herself. Another step upward was her gradution from a business college. This she accomplished without once asking her parents for tuition money. A third and major step toward her goal was a job she obtained, through her own initiative and wiles, as bookkeeper and typist in a large manufacturing concern.

Under normal circumstances, the best Marie could ever have expected in life was a petty clerkship or, more probably, menial service in the home of the well-to-do.

The Havlick couple were summoned to police headquarters. "Where had Marie obtained the money for all this schooling?" they were asked.

The mother would say nothing. The father hung his head and finally was induced to speak.

"Sirs, you know how hard life is for us poor," he told the officials. "Marie has beauty and grace. Naturally she attracted men. We could not control her—although often I beat her." He paused a second and wet his lips. Then:

"But she has nothing to do with this dreadful crime!"

More than that, on the subject of Marie's men friends, he would not say.

From neighbors of the Havlicks the police obtained more information about Marie. She had had many affairs—hence the father's cryptic remark that he often beat her. If these neighbors were to be believed, the girl was without sentimental interest in any of the men. She used them to acquire German, or to attend business, to get herself a job, to meet other men, to advance herself any way she could.

Ironically, she had not needed the aid of any of them to meet Judge Velgo. One day, in the Spring of 1934 she was sitting in the little park flanking the Svratka River. A middle-aged man of distinguished appearance sat down beside her.

"I beg your pardon. Have you a pencil?" he asked suavely.

It was the least subtle of pretexts to engage the girl in conversation. Not that Marie was backward, the woman neighbors insisted. Soon she determined that Judge Velgo should become her protector. He could be of more use to her than all his predecessors combined.

From a half dozen sources, police pieced together the rest of the story. Marie played the jurist with feline deliberation. She went to his apartment once, twice; she declared herself thrilled at the facility with which he played Chopin and Liszt. She even attended one of his sessions in the Circuit Court.

Then—she seemed to lose interest in him. For a month she refused to answer his notes or his appeals to her in the "personals" column of the papers; she would not acknowledge his flowers or his boxes of expensive candy.

Evidently her seeming indifference maddened the jurist into committing a fatal error. He begged, on bended knee, for her to marry him.

Marie's parents refused permission. They did not want to offend His Excellency, they said, but he—well, Marie was but a child, whereas His Excellency was 55. The difference, they pointed out, was too great.

Judge Velgo and Marie overcame their opposition. But from the parents the investigators learned that, anxious as he was to marry the Havlick daughter, the prominent jurist had not lost all sense of discretion. He insisted that the nuptials be solemnized at the unromantic hour of 6 in the morning.

In addition, he stipulated that not only must the cerecmony be kept secret, but that Marie must continue to live with her family.

The girl demurred at this, but Judge Velgo persisted. He explained that he had lived too long alone to feel comfortable living with another, even one as attractive as Marie. He promised that in a short while he would make a formal announcement of the marriage to his friends, but that it was impractical to reveal it at the present time.

Marie agreed. After all, she told herself, she would be the wife of a judge, with, in time, all the perquisites of that elevated station. She would have money, even though it was said the jurist was miserly. And, most important of all, the child that was coming would have a name.

The marriage was duly solemnized at St. Thomas' Church.

IT WAS evident to the police that Judge Velgo had planned to divorce the girl in a short time. It was also clear enough that he had married her for convenience.

But two events forestalled his

plans. One was the peasant-like shrewdness of the Havlicks, who, to force the jurist to take Marie into his home, expelled her from theirs. The other was, that soon after his marriage, he learned of a vacancy on the Supreme Court, and he hoped to be appointed to the post.

A divorce scandal, however, would automatically disqualify him for that important judicial office. He decided to bide his time.

Marie was now without a roof over her head. Because she was no longer living with her parents, the Judge held that the pre-nuptial agreement had been invalidated, and refused to give his wife money for food and shelter.

In desperation, Marie made a confidante of the Judge's washwoman. The latter was sympathetic. For a small sum, she said, she would put Marie in communication with an old friend of hers who might prove helpful. He had executed many delicate missions for others in trouble, the washwoman said, and was a most resourceful fellow.

The "resourceful fellow," the police ascertained, was Wenzel Cerny. The jurist's wife met him in an obscure cafe. He professed to be shocked at Judge Velgo's callous treatment of his wife.

"I know all about that husband of yours," Cerny exclaimed. "He's a rat! Two years ago he sent me to jail for six months for no reason except, perhaps, that he didn't like my looks. I'm not surprised," he added, "at the deal he's giving you. A scoundrel like that should be shot! . . . Have you any money?"

Cerny had planted an idea in Marie's pretty head. Under the Czech statutes her dowry rights would amount to two-thirds of her husband's estate. The immediate difficulty, however, was her lack of cash. Cerny demanded 20,000 kronen, or about $800.

She wheedled him down to 5,000 kronen.

The agreement between them was formalized by promissory note given to Cerny—a note composed by the pretty business college graduate that would have done credit to a financial genius or a shrewd lawyer. It read:

> "I hereby agree to pay you 5,000 kronen for services, the nature of which is only known to you, to me and to my husband (!). In case of my death, this obligation will be covered by a provision in my will. You incur obligation to talk to nobody about this agreement, to show it to nobody, and not to state your claims toward any third person. This debt may be collected neither in a legal way nor in any forcible way. In case of your death, your wife and your son inherit all your demands. The above amount may be paid in monthly or half yearly payments or

in one lump sum. Upon full payment, this note must be returned. In case of my being divorced, this promissory note becomes void."

The note bore the date of February 16, 1936. Precisely a month later, at about 10:20 P.M., the Press Bureau director in the apartment below Judge Velgo heard the commotion upstairs and summoned the police.

ON THE third day after the murder, the hospital director notified the police commandant that Cerny could talk—if he wanted to.

He did.

He said, bitterly, that he had no intention of shouldering all the blame, nor "of shielding that she-devil."

"Certainly I murdered Velgo! He got what was coming to him. If you don't believe the Havlick girl put me up to it, you'll find the promissory note sewn in the lining of my coat."

Just as Cerny had stated, the note was skilfully hidden where he said it was.

By a ruse, the police prevailed upon Marie to sign her name to a paper, explaining her signature was a necessary preliminary to an appeal for her release.

Next day they confronted the pretty widow with her signature on the promissory note, and the one she had just inscribed. They were identical.

Not till then did the girl abandon her story of a burglary, and confess to the Commandant that she was implicated in the murder plot.

"But," she said, "after giving that wretch the note, I had a change of heart, even though my husband had betrayed me. I could not see him shot down in cold blood. I tried to get my note back from Cerny. He refused.

"The night Judge Velgo was shot, I pleaded with Cerny not to go through with the horrible deed. He brushed me aside. When he heard my husband's key in the door, Cerny dragged me into the bedroom and threw me in the closet and locked the door. That's all I remember."

The trial of the pair on charges of murder opened on February 11, 1937. In view of her dowry prospects, Marie was able to obtain expert defense lawyers from Prague. They coached her carefully, and for the duration of the trial they dressed her in a mode that was demure and yet revealed her attractive figure.

Marie's legs and pretty knees were the most important exhibits the defense counsel introduced, so far as the jury could see.

After four days the jurors took the case. In 12 minutes they returned to the court-room, fatuous smiles on all their faces.

"We find the defendant Cerny guilty as charged!

"We find the defendant Marie

Havlick Velgo *not* guilty, in view of the irresistable force exercised upon her by the defendant Cerny."

Immediately the Court sentenced Cerny to 30 years' imprisonment at hard labor.

Marie Havlick Velgo walked from the courtroom a free woman. But her freedom was not to endure for long. The State Prosecutor moved for a new trial on grounds of improper evidence introduced by the defense. The press took his part, ridiculing the jury in wrathy editorials, and asserting that its members had been moved, not by the judicial evidence but by the evidence of Marie's charms.

A second trial was granted the state, and Marie was again arrested and lodged in the Brno penitentiary. While there she gave birth to a daughter, who she claimed, was the child of the murdered judge. The child was allowed to remain with her in the cell until the trial was called in October, 1937. The baby was then made the ward of the slain jurist's brother.

This time the defense was more aggressive. Instead of displaying a comely, dimpled widow with pretty knees for the jury's contemplation, Marie's lawyers concentrated their attack on the murdered man himself. They introduced, as exhibits, the judge's diary in which he recounted his affairs, in erotic tones, with scores of young girls to whom he had "lent" small sums.

The young widow's lawyers argued that wedded life with the Circuit Court Justice, who was painted as a Czechoslovak equivalent of a Dr. Jekyll and Mr. Hyde, was intolerable to a girl of delicate instincts.

But the hard-headed jury, remembering Marie's previous *affairs d'amour,* and impervious to her dimples, found her guilty. And the girl of "delicate instincts" was sentenced to 12 years' imprisonment.

How to Capture Bank Robbers

ONE of the most unusual clues to lead to the capture of five New Jersey hold-up men, was found near the scene of a recent Newark bank robbery.

Detective Sergeant Joseph Kenney was detailed to solve the case. The next day, after the hold-up, he brought in five men who took part in the crime.

Sergeant Kenney, explaining the capture, revealed the following interesting item:

"A few days before the robbery, a suspicious-looking car was seen near the bank. *Someone had the presence of mind to write down the license number on a wall.* Checking with the License Bureau at Trenton, we got the name of the owner of the car. The rest was easy."

Approximately $13,000 taken in the robbery, was recovered.

TERROR IN THE UKRAINE

By

Ivan Petrienov

OVER a deeply furrowed road cutting the windswept plains of western Russia, a Ford of ancient vintage pushed doggedly through the night.

Filled with a nameless dread, the driver, one I. Kushmin, a traveling salesman, clung to the wheel, bracing himself against a gale that threatened to overturn the old car.

The lights of the venerable Model T intermittently flared and dimmed as he eased it over the frozen ruts. Unless he could soon reach his destination, the hamlet of Lissino, he would be marooned by threatening snowdrifts.

A few miles from the village the road became smoother; the headlights brightened and threw a

RUSSIA: *Particles of dust found on a decorative side-comb leads to the capture of a terrorist gang that had murdered over 200 peasants. One of the best examples of crime detection.*

steady beam. Suddenly, some yards ahead, they revealed a human figure lying in the middle of the road.

At that eerie moment, with the wind howling around the machine, Kushmin jammed on the brakes and brought his shuddering car to a stop.

With head and body bent against the wind, he fought his way to the huddled form.

"My God!" he muttered, as he leaned over it, "it's a girl. Look at the blood!"

The girl was bleeding profusely from a deep gash over her right eye, and apparently was still alive. Picking her up in his arms, Kushmin staggered back to the Ford. He placed her in the rear with his samples and sped on through the roaring elements for Lissino.

IT WAS after midnight when Kushmin reached the snoring village. The sole light came from the bleak shack housing the militia post. He rushed into the small building and stuttered his tale to E. Martianov, the local police chief. Together they carried the girl indoors. The officer washed the blood from her face, and placed her on the floor, near the pot-bellied stove.

Once they had bathed her head, the chief of police and the frightened salesman saw a beautiful face; framed by golden hair.

"It's Maria Smirnova!" Martianov exclaimed. "I know her family well. How far from the farmhouse did you find her? Did you see any lights?"

Kushmin explained he had not investigated. Frankly, he was terrified, he said, and had thought it best to hurry the girl to Lissino.

Martianov called the nearest doctor to care for Maria, and placed Kushmin in the custody of an aide. "Maybe you're telling the truth," he addressed the chagrined salesman, "but you'll have to wait until I return." Then the police chief aroused three of his men and drove rapidly off in the direction of the Smirnova farm, three miles away.

There were no lights showing anywhere and the men had difficulty locating the Smirnova place until scudding clouds momentarily revealed the moon, and they saw the silhouette of the house and out-buildings.

The lights of the police car were turned into the farmyard and, with lamps lit, the men advanced. Two of them had their revolvers at the ready.

They were first confronted with the body of Farmer Smirnova, lying in a grotesque posture near the door of the house.

"He's stone dead!" one of the awed officers cried after a brief examination. "Been stabbed in the back, shot through the neck and struck over the head. Looks like the work of terrorists!"

The quartet, now all with revolvers in hand, rushed the house and, with Martianov in the lead, dashed through the door.

The rays of their swinging lamps revealed a scene of unspeakable gruesomeness.

The farmer's wife and his 80-year-old mother were lashed back-to-back in two chairs, the soles of their feet burned to the bone. There was the nauseating smell of scorched flesh.

Both women had been shot several times, stabbed in a dozen places and beaten over the head, in the same manner as the dead farmer. Both, of course, were lifeless.

Even the police, accustomed to scenes of violence, were sickened. But worse was to come.

Near one of the windows they found the bodies of Smirnova's two small sons, their little heads cleanly split by an ax. They lay in a widening pool of blood.

In a corner, lying beneath a table, Martianov found still another body, that of a man who had been shot in the abdomen.

"What else in this charnel-house!" the police chief exclaimed. "This man is dead too. He's Pjotr Rumin, the young manager of our co-operative in Lissino. The gossips say he was engaged to Maria Smirnova."

The chief of police lost no time. He barked orders to his men to look for fingerprints and instructed them to determine if anything had been stolen, although he doubted that simple theft could be the motive for the wholesale murders. It seemed more probable that it was the work of one or more madmen who harbored a grudge against the farmer and his family.

MARTIANOV'S first move on returning to the police barracks was to send the coroner to the farmhouse, accompanied by a photographer who would take pictures of the murder-scene and the positions of the bodies. Thus a permanent record would be had for the purpose of reconstructing the crimes.

Next he phoned to every militia station within a radius of 100 miles and asked that all suspicious characters riding or tramping the roads be held for questioning.

The militia were quick to co-operate and posses of men and boys were hurriedly recruited. Those that were armed were ordered to beat their way through the forest where it might be supposed the murderer or murderers would hide.

The chief hurried to the home of the doctor who had Maria in care; the remote hamlet having nothing that resembled a hospital.

"She must live," he told the doctor. "Remember — there are six dead back there, and the girl is the only eye-witness!"

The doctor shrugged.

"I don't dare hazard a guess. She's had a terrific blow over the head. Her delirium suggests brain fever, which is usually fatal. But I'll do my best."

Meanwhile the posses beating through the country-side had encountered no one they could hold for more than a few hours. The few wandering peddlers all had foolproof alibis, and their papers were in order. Kushmin, the traveling salesman, was released. There was nothing to link him with the murders. Whoever had committed the horrible crimes had slipped away.

Thirty-six hours after the girl had been found, she was still unconscious and rapidly sinking.

For the moment, the only clues consisted of a large number of fingerprints, bullets and shells that had been found in the blood-splattered home of the Smirnovas. These had been promptly forwarded to the Moscow laboratories of the MOUR, the Moskovski Ougolvni Rosisk, attached to the Soviet Department of Criminal Investigation.

Chief Martianov now began a minute inquiry into the lives of the Smirnovas. Everyone testified that the farmer and his family were well-liked; that he had had no disputes with any of his neighbors. Rumin, the young manager of the co-operative, was also respected in the community and had no enemies. There was no question of any quarrel between him and other suitors for Maria's hand.

At this stage of the investigation, the girl died without having uttered one intelligible word. She had been incoherent in her delirium and the harrassed police could make nothing of her pitiful gibbirish.

CHIEF MARTIANOV now made another discovery. Because police had originally found a few articles missing, they believed that these might have been removed to mislead the investigation. However, when neighbors who knew the Smirnovas intimately were brought to the scene, they called the attention of the police to a long list of stolen property, thus clearly establishing the motive for the murders.

The robbers had removed virtually everything save the house and out-buildings. Almost all the stock in the barn—the two cows, three pigs and all the chickens—had disappeared. They had even carted off a hand-carved cradle.

Because of the particularly revolting character of the crime, Chief Martianov was superseded in authority by two special investigators from MOUR—Inspectors Vladimir and Tchernigov, who were considered the best men in the Department of Criminal Investigation at Moscow.

With Martianov and his aides, they huddled around the red-hot stove in the militia post at Lissino. After reviewing the case and exchanging information, the Moscow operatives turned to the reports on the fingerprints.

"We can't trace them to any known criminals," Vladimir admitted. "That means our task will be so much more difficult. But," he continued, "we're not without any clues. It's clear from the type and caliber of the shells and bullets found at the Smirnova's that they were fired from army ordnance, that is, from Schneider-Creuzct and Putilev revolvers."

"Which means," Inspector Tchernigov interrupted "that we're fairly sure the men — for there unquestionably had to be more than one—were former soldiers who have deserted with their equipment."

"That's a pretty slender clue," Martianov observed.

"That's true," Vladimir conceded, "but we know this: what we must track down is one of those nomadic gangs of ex-soldiers and escaped prisoners who are running wild over the country-side and terrorizing the people.

"For example, we know that there must have been at least six or eight men, because a lesser number could not carry away all the stuff that was stolen. It's likely too, that several among them still wore their army caps.

"And most important of all, we know that eventually most of the loot will turn up in one or more pawn-shops. When that happens, we'll be getting close, even if the gang, as is likely, disposes of the clothes and other things through a fence."

The two Moscow inspectors went about their job methodically. They first took a map and drew concentric circles extending to a radius of 800 kilometers, about 500 miles, from Lissino. A number of large towns and a few cities were embraced within these circles. The police of all these communities were warned to be on the alert for the following:

1. Any men found to possess army revolvers.

2. Any men wearing army caps or other military clothing.

3. Any men attempting to sell the articles stolen from the Smirnovas.

A list of stolen articles was furnished to all the militia within the radius mapped out by the inspectors.

Before returning to Moscow to direct the man-hunt from that central point, the inspectors reconstructed the crime as best they might from the photographs taken at the scene of the murders, showing, in detail, the position of the bodies and the condition of the room. Thus they were able to make out the following report:

ON A winter evening early in 1935, the Smirnova family was at dinner in the large room that served as living-room, kitchen and dining-room.

The farmer sat at the head of the rough pine table. At the other end sat his wife, presiding over the huge bowl of *borscht*. On the farmer's left sat Maria, doubtless clasping beneath the table the hand of young Rumin, seated at her right.

On the other side of the table sat Smirnova's old mother, and ranged to her left were the two small boys.

The hour must have been about seven, for the food had not been entirely consumed.

The farmer's aged mother, known by neighbors to be particularly nervous, and beset by all manner of fears and superstitions, was seated closest to the door.

Doubtless she was the first to hear a noise in the darkness outside, and asked her son to investigate. Presumably, the farmer left the table to satisfy his frightened parent. His indulgence of his mother's whim cost him his life, for, as he stepped outside he was attacked.

A few seconds thereafter the door was opened violently—it was partly unhinged when the police arrived.

An upturned chair near the door suggested that Rumin had courageously hurled it at the intruders. Evidently he was killed by a bullet fired from the door.

The two little boys apparently had jumped from their seats, retreated around the table and hidden behind Maria's voluminous skirts, for their bodies were found where the girl usually sat at mealtimes.

Then the bandits trussed up the old mother and her daughter-in-law in two chairs, and burned their feet to make them reveal where their money was hidden.

Neighbors knew the Smirnovas did not keep cash on the premises. Unquestionably, when the two terrified women failed to disclose their non-existent cache of rubles, they were shot and stabbed.

Meanwhile, so far as the inspectors could reason, Maria had fled outside, hoping to summon aid. One of the bandits, possibly a lookout man left by the farm gate, seized her and struck the frenzied girl down. Later, when the bandits had left, she revived and made her way down the road, only to collapse on the spot where Kushmin came upon her in his car.

Finally, because the two small boys were squealing with terror, and the bandits feared that a peasant passing on the road might raise the alarm, their heads were split by an ax.

With all their victims disposed of, the gang gathered up all they could carry and fled into the night.

But to where? And how soon and in what manner would the assassins give themselves away? Their apprehension would demand smart police work.

THE CHIEFS of the Department of Criminal Investigation, far from the scene of the crime, decided the wisest move was to make it appear that the inquiry into the murders was closed.

Newspapers throughout the country were instructed to publish a notice to the effect that the murders at Lissino "had been committed by a person or persons unknown."

Moreover, to give the bandits a further false sense of security, the police in all the communities were instructed to remove the bulletin-board circulars which had vaguely described the desperadoes. The newspaper stories also added that the reward, which had been offered for their capture, had been rescinded.

The reason for these moves was that the MOUR believed the best chance of trapping the men was through the pawn-shops. Until the investigation appeared to be closed the bandits would not dare sell the stolen goods.

But weeks were to pass before the first break came.

Nearly three months later a Moscow plain clothesman was making a routine tour of the pawnshops, seeking stolen goods. In one of the poorer districts of the capital he came across a peasant's sheepskin windbreaker for sale.

"That's not a bad garment, Comrade," the detective remarked to the shopkeeper. "How much? I'm a poor man."

The owner named a price.

"Tell me, Comrade, where did it come from?" the detective asked perfunctorily.

"Oh, I've forgotten," answered the shopkeeper irritably. "What difference does it make? D'you want it, or don't you? I'll knock off a ruble if you'll take it now!"

It seemed to the detective that the man was over-eager to get rid of the coat. He knew that one like it had been stolen from the Smirnova farm, although that was not necessarily a clue: thousands of such garments are worn by Russian peasants.

As the detective repeatedly turned over the coat, the shopowner became more and more annoyed. "If you don't want it, get out!" he cried. "I'm busy. Be off!"

Once the detective identified himself, however, the man showed his alarm. Obediently he brought out the record of purchases that police regulations demand of pawnbrokers.

"Here it is," he whined. "My record shows that I bought the windbreaker from a woman named Ljuba Kazin. She's sold me stuff before. But don't blame me, Comrade. I'm an honest man."

"Never mind about that. Where does this Kazin woman live?"

"Sukharevskaya 23."

"Very well. And I'll take the coat along! If you're lying, you'd better get out of Moscow—if you can!"

The pawnbroker obsequiosly opened the door for the detective, meanwhile protesting his innocence.

Photographs were sent posthaste to Lissino. There, neighbors were reasonably certain that it had belonged to Smirnova. The importance of this discovery was that it gave a clue in what locality the bandits may have disposed of the remainder of the loot.

The police went through other Moscow pawn-shops with a fine-toothed comb, as it were. Although Lissino residents could not definitely swear to the ownership of the coat, there was no question of the origin of a hand-carved crib the detectives found in another pawn-shop, not very distant from the one where the windbreaker had been uncovered.

"What did I tell you!" Vladimir exulted to Tchernigov. "I'll bet a bottle of *vodka* to a bowl of soup, the gang's right here in Moscow. Let's question this Kazin woman!"

Ljuba Kazin, however, could not be found.

Made restive by the redoubled surveillance of the police, the pawnbrokers agreed to aid the authorities as far as they could.

"Yes," many of them agreed, "we know her from your description. But she didn't give us that name. She generally comes in with a heavy-set, muscular man of about 40. We never had any reason to suspect her. She has sold us various things, like many of the poor."

The woman, police determined, had used a score of names. They picked up her trail in dozens of pawn-shops, but it led nowhere.

The authorities now applied greater pressure on the pawnbrokers. They threatened them with even more stringent State regulations if the flat-nosed Ljuba Kazin were not found. After waiting two days, Inspector Vladimir at the MOUR headquarters received a telephone call.

"That woman's here now," the caller whispered over the phone. "My shop is at 47 .... I'll keep her here, with her male companion, as long as I can—but hurry!"

Inspectors Vladimir and Tchernigov raced to the shop. They ordered another police car to remain several yards ahead of them and, at Vladimir's signal, to arrest the couple.

The man and the woman emerged from the pawn-shop and headed for the new Moscow subway.

Vladimir signalled to the detectives in the car ahead. One of them stepped from the machine, a few feet from the entrance of the subway, and grabbed the man by the arm.

The woman's companion turned swiftly and stunned the detective by a blow on the head with his cane.

The couple raced down the steps and into a train that somehow, miraculously, was just ready to pull out of the station.

As Inspector Tchernigov, racing after the fleeing couple, reached the station platform, the train was already moving. He picked up the station-agent's emergency phone and ordered the dispatcher at the next stop to delay the train.

Nevertheless, the mysterious pair managed to elude the police.

THE two inspectors in charge of the man-hunt were more than disgusted. Evidently all their weeks of painstaking work had gone for nothing. As far as they were concerned, they were back at the point where they had started, with the added handicap that the woman would no longer dare visit any more pawn-shops.

But they had one clue, although a slender one. Near the point where the detective had been struck over the head by the woman's companion, a decorative side-comb was found on the sidewalk. The ingenious MOUR laboratories found, after long study, that it bore a fine covering of cement dust.

Thus, the police deduced, the woman might live in some neighborhood where construction was underway. The quality of the dust indicated that it came from cement used in the building of model tenements.

Two such tenements, police learned, were under construction about five blocks from the pawnshop where the woman and her companion had last appeared.

The next step was to go through dwellings in that quarter. They called on the superintendents of at least 50 old apartment houses. But there was no trace of the two fugitives.

"We're wasting our time," Inspector Vladimir told his partner. "If this Ljuba Kazin woman is a fence—and there's no doubt she is—she wouldn't be living in an apartment with the stolen stuff she's bought. For one thing there wouldn't be room."

"And for another," Tchernigov agreed, "all that stuff coming to any flat would arouse the suspicions of neighbors. So—what then?"

Vladimir thought a moment before speaking.

"The answer must be she lives in a loft. Someplace away from prying eyes, where she can get her stolen goods brought in at night. And where there's room for it."

This sounded logical enough and the inspectors began looking for lofts in the neighborhood of the model-tenements. Eventually they reached a block of old loft-buildings on Lesnaya Ulitza.

In the areaway flanking the buildings, the investigators found a covering of fine dust that had sifted down from the new tenements rising a few yards away.

The dust here was identical in quality with that on the side-comb dropped by the woman!

Reinforced by five detectives, Vladimir led a search through the loft-structures. One of the storage suites into which they broke, had been leased by a man named Palski. Here the triumphant detectives neared the end of their trail.

The rooms were filled with loot reported stolen from farmers in the Moscow regions and from residents of the capital itself.

The investigators hid behind the piles of expensive furniture, trunks and boxes that filled the storerooms to overflowing.

Late that evening, a woman and a man walked into the hideaway. The latter was easily disarmed and, after a long grilling by Vladimir, the pair decided to tell what they knew. They had used a variety of names, they said, but their real ones were Anatol Ulkinshk and Rebecca Zebstein.

"Yes," the woman finally admitted, "we had some of the goods that was stolen from the Smirnova's, as you say, but we didn't know it. It came to us from other fences connected with the Kotov gang."

"Where do they hide out?" Vladimir was quick to ask.

"In the Ukraine."

Vladimir and Tchernigov exchanged glances of despair. The Ukraine—750 miles from Moscow, a vast region dotted by stretches of almost impenetrable forests!

WEARILY, the two inspectors set off for the Ukraine, that vast wheat-bowl of Russia. For weeks they worked with the police of a score of provincial communities, and pursued a thousand fruitless clues.

But at last their diligent efforts were rewarded. After many months since the Smirnova massacre, they traced the Kotov gang to their hideaway.

The bandits occupied a delapidated shack not far from the village of Niekine. Their defenses consisted of a thick encircling forest as dense as the Congo. It took the converging police-force a day and a night to make its way through the tangle to within a few yards of the cabin.

Equipped with revolvers, machine-guns and hand-grenades, they waited for dawn to rush the hideout.

As Inspector Vladimir crept forward at the head of his men, a girl emerged from the shack, pail in hand. She advanced toward the well, then, hearing the sound of trampled underbrush, screamed and darted back to the house.

Instantly, gun-fire burst out on all sides.

In the first fusillade, the relentless Inspector Vladimir, the human bloodhound who had traced the Smirnova butchers from Lissino to Moscow to Niekine in the Ukraine, fell with a bullet through his chest.

Tchernigov held up a hand as

an order to his men to lie low. Recklessly exposing himself, he set up one of the machine-guns. At his signal the general firing began and the shack was soon riddled by bullets.

The gang endured this devastating hail of lead for another ten minutes until Tchernigov, with superb aim, hurled a grenade through a broken window of the fortress. Then the police rushed the ruins.

Within, the attackers found a score of men and women screaming with pain. A number were dead; not one had escaped unwounded.

The Kotov terrorists were quickly disarmed. They had no stomach for further resistance. But the man who had led the long chase, Inspector Vladimir, did not see the actual capture. He died where he had fallen.

IN THE rear of the Central Correctional Institute of Moscow, a group of men and women were lined up against a stained and bullet-pitted wall. The vicious crack of a dozen rifles executed all but Kotov. He had not been lined up with the other blindfolded terrorists. The MOUR director had reserved him for the gentle offices of the grieving Tchernigov.

Tchernigov drilled the bandit through the right eye with Vladimir's automatic.

A Sticky Escape

GUARDS at Sing Sing Prison have learned to avoid foreign entanglements. Two aliens, Gus Kindt, Belgian locksmith, and John DeLeon, Spanish glazier, determined to escape. Confined in a cell on an upper tier, they knew that the two night guards ate their meals at the northern end of the gallery. Having managed to unlock their cell-door with false keys, they quietly turned out two lights and crept along the gallery toward the guards. Having gone as far as they dared without attracting attention, they papered the gallery floor with sticky fly-paper for several feet, and then fled.

As the guards, attracted by the noise of running feet, chased after the fleeing prisoners, they plunged into the adhesive paper, stolen from the kitchen. Soon, their shoes and trousers were hopelessly involved in the sticky mess, slowing up their progress to such an extent that the foreigners were able to reach a ground floor window with time to spare. The prisoners spread bars they had previously sawed almost through, climbed out and escaped.

MOONSHINE MADNESS

By

Leon Andrews

U. S. A.: *When George Pingley sold some innocent sheep for slaughter, he knew they were going to die; but little did he realize that they would put him in the shadow of the electric chair.*

SQUINTING along the well-polished rifle barrel, the gaunt mountaineer took careful aim at the saucy little squirrel that was eyeing him from the tree branch. He was just about to pull the trigger when his companion excitedly said:

"Wait — don't shoot now, George!"

His aim spoiled by the suddenness of the remark, George Pingley turned with a snarl.

"Why not?" he demanded.

"Because, there's th' sheriff!"

Pingley looked toward the road, partly hidden by the dense woods of the desolate wooded section of Frederick County, in the northernmost corner of Virginia.

"Why—that—!" he snarled, a fierce look of hatred clouding his evil-visaged face, heightened by a two-day growth of black and wiry whiskers. "No dad-rat sheriff is goin' tuh take me!"

"Wonder what he's talkin' to Ernie Nesselrodt about? He in trouble?"

"Who—Ernie in trouble? Naw! Sheriff Newcome uses him to pry out things. Why, just th' other day, he offered Ernie $10 if he'd tell him where my still is, back there! But Ernie is a good boy; he wouldn't tell. Fine worker, too. Asked him tuh do some chores for me when I went up to Wardensville last week, but he's gott'n himself a job . . . "

Pingley continued to stare at Sheriff Newcome and the 18-year-old mountain youth, a laborer on farms in the area of Mt. Williams, where he lived, and Mountain Falls, the home town of Pingley.

"Ain't got no truck with that sheriff," mused Pingley, aloud. "I don't owe him a thing, and he don't owe me anything—so why don't he leave me be? Ain't as though I was the only man in these hills who made his own likker! Best corn-squeezin's in this or any other county, too!"

Clarence Sine—who, with his brothers George and Ben—lived in a cabin a short distance from Pingley and who helped him distill the famous Virginia hill country "mountain dew", — wrinkled his weather-beaten brow and regarded his companion quizzically.

"Sure it's the still that Newcome's after? Isn't there some other trouble you're in, George?"

"Waal, there's that little business about'n the sheep—"

"The ones you sold?"

"Yeah. But they was mine, wasn't they? Why shouldn't I sold them?"

"I swear, I don't understand much about this law business, George; but it appears you couldn't sell them legal-like—"

"Dagnab the law! It's crazy, that's what it is!"

Sine chuckled. "You ought to know—you been mixed up enough with it!"

Pingley glared at his friend.

"If you're alludin' to that time I went up tuh Blanton Orndorff's house with Deputy George Baggeant, an' Mrs. Orndorff was killed in the scuffle—fergit it! Didn't those newspaper-writin' fellers say it was a mystery? Well, that's what it is, see? And the law had nothin' to do with it—"

"I wasn't thinkin' so much about that, George," drawled Sine. "I was thinkin' of that ruckus you had in that poolroom battle at Strasburg—"

"Aw! That?"

The splutter of the sheriff driving off in his car broke up the conversation. Pingley waited until he had jounced out of sight on the rough country road, and then called out to Nesselrodt.

"Hey, Ernie! C'mere!"

The youth looked up, startled, then scrambled through the tangled brush into the small clearing where the mountaineers had been trying to fill a stew-pot with squirrels.

"What's Newcome after now—my still again?" demanded Pingley.

"No, he's got a paper for you—it's those sheep!"

"What about 'em?"

" 'Pears as though you have to turn over the $400 you got for 'em or go tuh jail."

"Jail!" snorted Pingley contemptuously. "Not me! Not while Sheriff Newcome is the jailer. It's bad enough livin' in the same county with him, let alone livin' under the same roof, because you know he lives in th' jail, too. I couldn't take even a day of it!"

"Sheriff says it means 10 years —" the youth put in.

"Ten years!" exclaimed Pingley with such a loud roar that it set some birds twittering excitedly in the leaf-less February trees. "He can't do that to me!"

"Says he's a-goin' to, though," the boy said solemnly.

"He's just talkin' big . . . why, that—!"

"Why don't you go away, George," counselled Sine, "until this thing peters itself out? You got some kinfolk just a few miles away over there in West Virginia. You could go there. Newcome couldn't touch you."

"Me run away?" Pingley was scornful. "Not me! No sir! I got as much right tuh stay right here in Frederick County as Newcome has. More, I reckon—my grandpappy's pappy built my house and Newcome — he ain't even got a house! Lives in the jail!"

"Guess you're right, George!"

"Sure I'm right!"

"Let's pot some squirrels," suggested Sine. "It's gettin' late."

Mumbling to himself, Pingley tucked his shotgun under his arm and strode off ahead of the others.

"Sheriff Newcome sure has him upset," whispered Sine to the youth.

The boy grinned. "Sure has," he said.

EARLY on the evening of the same day—February 13, 1938—Sheriff J. William Newcome, who had been appointed to that office in March, 1937, reached the end of his patience in trying to apprehend the huge mountaineer. He decided to ask the co-operation of the Virginia State police.

Phoning State Trooper R. E. Bayliss, the sheriff informed him that he had a warrant for the arrest of Pingley on charges of selling 51 sheep on which George R. Green held a lien.

"I've got to bring him in for a trial on a felony charge before Trial Justice A. J. Travener—and they want to know what the delay is," the sheriff added. "Can you or one of the troopers help me out?"

"Sure—glad to," Bayliss replied. "You know the State officers are always ready to give a hand to local and county police."

"Fine," said Newcome. "I'll come over and pick you up at the Winchester police station tonight about 8 o'clock."

"I don't think I can make it tonight — have some other duties. Why not make it tomorrow?"

"Well, I'd like to have him fresh and handy in court tomorrow morning," chuckled the sheriff.

"That's up to you. If I'm not here, somebody will be around."

"Thanks."

At the appointed time, Sheriff Newcome strode into the police station. He was a big man, weighing almost 200 pounds, and his heavy step caused the chairs in the reception room to jiggle.

George F. Miller, of the Virginia Highway police, and Policeman Edwin Smith, of the local Winchester force, abruptly cut off their conversation and smiled at the sheriff.

"Evenin', Bill," greeted Miller. "Looking for somebody?"

"Bayliss," said the sheriff, easing himself into a chair. "Is he around?"

"No; he was called out. Anything I can do?"

Newcome tilted back comfortably in the chair and eyed Miller in his natty uniform, and Smith, who was off duty and in civilian clothes. "Yes," drawled the sheriff, "I want to go out to Mountain Falls and bring in Pingley—"

"Pingley? Is he in trouble again?" asked Smith, who had several encounters with the mountaineer when he visited the town on periodic sprees.

"Is he ever out of it?" shot back the sheriff with a laugh. Then, "Bayliss said there'd be someone here who could go out with me and help bring him in. I've been trying to lay my hands on him for more'n a week now, but he's going around boasting to those hill cronies of his that I can't get him."

"Oh! Tough, is he?" exclaimed Miller, understandingly.

"Thinks he is," Newcome replied. "The law means nothing to him or to any of that bunch up there in the woods. Well, Miller—would you like to come along with me? Not that I don't think I could handle him by myself—I'm as big as he is, and I'll match my 45 years with his any day. But I might need a little door guarding, or something . . . "

"Sure," Miller agreed. Turning to Smith, he said, "Want to come along for the ride, Smitty?"

"Why not?" Smith agreed, "I've got nothing better to do right now."

"It's a fine warm night—more like June than February — and there's a big moon that will help us on our drive, which shows a moon's good for something besides romance," laughed Newcome, winking at the young and handsome Smith.

As the trio bounced over the rough mountain roads they discussed Pingley and his wild hill country brood. A few miles from Mountain Falls the car neared the home of Laban Hodgson, Mountain Falls mail carrier and day laborer.

"I think I'll ask Laban if he knows if Pingley's home," said the sheriff. "He may be back in the hills, 'working' with his pals. Nice night for some quiet brewin'!"

His companions laughed at the

sally as the sheriff eased himself out of the car and went up and pounded on the door. In a minute it was flung open by Hodgson.

"How are you, Laban?" asked Newcome neighborly. "Can you tell me if Pingley is home?"

Hodgson scratched the nape of his neck, musingly. "I can't be certain, sheriff. But leastwise, I don't know where he'd go at this time of night. I saw him in the village this afternoon—"

"Did he say anything about me looking for him?"

"Did he! He was a-cussin' all up and down about you!"

"He's trying to dodge me, isn't he?"

"Well, he sorta made it plain he was keepin' out of your way. Had a lot of fancy names he didn't learn from no parson that he was callin' you."'

Newcome laughed. "Thanks, Laban. G'night!"

Returning to the police car, Newcome told his companions that Pingley probably could be found at his home.

"We'll grab him easy," he said confidently. "No trouble at all."

"Did you expect trouble?" asked Miller.

"Why should I?" countered Newcome. "He's not a dangerous criminal, snoozin' with a gun under his pillow and one eye open, like these city gang fellers. He'll listen to reason and come along as sweet as honey, you'll see, despite his natural cussedness."

"But what if he doesn't," asked Smith from the back seat.

"There are three of us, aren't there—and only one of him."

"Well, if there is trouble, I'm out of luck. I don't pack a gun when I'm in my street duds!"

"You won't need a gun—there'll be no shooting," assured Newcome. "There's his cabin now—"

UP on a hill rose the odd-shaped ancestral log-cabin of the Pingley clan. The rear of the main house—to which a second shack-like building had been attached as the family grew and prospered in its hill-billy way—was a slope to which the outside stairs descended. From a big outer chimney attached to the larger section of the house issued a thin string of smoke. But there were no lights in any of the windows.

"Guess they're asleep," said Miller.

"Good!" grunted Newcome. "We'll rouse 'em out of bed. Pingley will be more likely to listen to reason if he's still got cobwebs in that brain o' his. Come on!"

The three officers quietly crept up from the highway to the ungainly dwelling. Reaching a cleared space at the side of the house, Newcome gave his instructions.

"Miller, you watch the side door here. Smitty, you go around to the back, and if Pingley tries to sneak out and get into the hills, you shout blue-murder! Now, we don't want any rough stuff."

"Okay," chorused the officers, starting off to their respective posts.

Newcome called Smith back. "Here's a searchlight—you might need it: looks kinda dark back there. The hill hides the moon. I have another light in my pocket."

"Thanks," said Smith, taking the electric torch. "It'll make a good club, if nothing else."

"You won't need it for that," assured the sheriff, striding toward the front door.

In a second his fist was resounding against the wooden panel.

"Pingley!" he shouted. "Come out!"

There was a deep silence. Again the sheriff pounded, called and kicked the door with his heavy boot. "Pingley—it's the law!"

Suddenly, Officer Miller summoned the sheriff to the side of the house where he had been standing on tip-toe and peering into the window. The room was pitch-dark.

"I think I saw someone moving in there!" he said.

The sheriff peered through the unwashed glass.

"You got good eyes!" said the sheriff. "What you saw is a pot of plants—and there's no breeze in there to move 'em!"

"Bill, I'm positive I saw something move in there!" Miller swore. Then, "How about trying this side door—it might be open."

"I'll try it," said Newcombe. "You go around to the front and watch, in case Pingley tries to slip away."

The sheriff pounded, demanding entrance as Miller slipped to the front. Again there was silence, and Newcome tried the handle. The door, securely barred from the inside, refused to budge.

Cursing under his breath, Newcome strode around to the rear and mounted the steep back porch steps. Once more he banged his heavy fist against the door, and kicked mightily.

"Pingley!" he cried out angrily. "Come down here!"

Smith, watching him from his point of vantage in the cluttered yard, asked, "Want me to help you break down the door?"

Newcome grunted in answer, and placed his shoulder against the stout pine. He felt it give. Smith started up the steps to help him when suddenly Newcome twisted the handle. The door was unlocked, and swung open easily.

"Doggone!" said the sheriff, in surprise.

Walking into the dark kitchen and stumbling over a stool, the sheriff went to the foot of the stairs leading into the upper part of the house.

"Pingley—come down, or I'll come up and fetch you!"

There was an electric silence. Then Newcome heard a heavy board give a dismal creak, as though someone was walking upon it in stocking feet. Sure, now, that someone was up there, Newcome slowly started up the steps.

A FEW minutes later a slim form came scampering down the rear steps. In the moonlight, Officer Smith recognized Harry Pingley, young son of the mountaineer.

Without glancing at the officer, the youth kicked his way across the yard in his slippered feet and went to the woodpile. Selecting a log, he stood it up against the chopping block and picked up the ax. He started to split the short log into kindling.

"Here, you need more light—you'll whack off a toe," said Smith, sauntering over toward the boy and playing his flashlight beam upon the chopping block.

The boy only grunted.

"What's the idea, chopping wood this time of night?" asked Smith.

"Fire's gone out," said the boy.

"Did you see Sheriff Newcome?"

"Yeah."

"What's he doing in there?"

"You know what he's doin'!"

There was silence a minute while the lad split some more kindling. Finally he said, "That ol' Sheriff! Can't let a body sleep. An' me sick, too—"

"What's the matter with you?"

"Sore throat. That's why I want the fire—to get hot water and keep warm." Carefully the boy massaged his Adam's apple, as though to ease the pain of talking.

"Sure taking a long time for the sheriff to bring your father down," remarked Smith, gazing at the house. He was facing a blank wall, and could not see whether the lamps had been lit or not. The boy went on with his task, coughing now and then. At last he said, "You better start to move, there's goin' to be Cain raised 'round here—"

"What's that—?"

"Pop ain't gonna be taken—he'll raise Ole Ned with that Newcome fella afore he's through."

Smith laughed. "I don't think so," he said reassuringly.

"You don't, eh? Well, that's why I got out of'n the way! I wa'nt goin' stay around up there. Pop, he's got 'nough 'dew' in 'im now to rassle a pa'ssle o' wildcats. No town sheriff goin' to stand in his way. Especially after what that Newcome did up there in the sleepin' room!"

"What did he do?" asked Smith, showing alarm.

"Waal—I was a-sleepin' on a cot down at the end of Mom's big bed 'cause there was a fire in that room. Mom an' Sis was a-sleepin' in the bed, quiet 'n' peaceful as anything. Suddenly, this here Newcome comes a-creapin' up the steps. He sticks a light in my face 'n' asks where Pop is. He shows me a paper, sayin' as how the paper says he's got to lay the hands o' the law on Pop . . . "

"Yes—?"

"I says 'tweren't none o' my business. Then the Sheriff steps aroun' to where Mom and Sis is lyin' under the covers. Sheriff says:

'Come out of there, Pingley!' Guess he thought 'twas Mom 'n' Pop there in the bed. Nobody moves. So—" the boy started coughing. "Sure sore to talk this way," he said.

"So what then?" prompted Smith.

"Waal, the sheriff takes the blankets and yanks 'em clean off'n the bed—*swissh!* like that! There was Mom, scairt as a rabbit, and Sis—well, Sis, she don't sleep in nothin' but a pair o' them slick silk pants like girls wear—" the youth chortled, rather amused—"and then I sees Pop come stalkin' in, like a cat after a sparrow-bird. Now, yuh know, no sheriff ain't goin' come aroun' our house a-doin' things like that—Pop won't stand for it, even when he ain't full o' corn squeezin's!"

Suddenly—as though the boy's words were prophetic—there was a terrific racket in the house, with sounds of cursing and the scuffling of heavy feet on the bare pine floor.

Then the thunderous roar of a gun and the shriek of a man mortally wounded. The door flew open, and Sheriff Newcome toppled head first onto the porch.

"George! Get him, George!" Newcome called to Miller, then was silent.

Miller, who had stationed himself a short distance from the house, so as to be able to watch both the front and side doors in case the giant mountaineer attempted to escape, ran to the porch, his service revolver in hand. As he reached the top landing of the verandah, he ordered Pingley to surrender.

The hillman's son and Smith watched on, horrified. They heard Miller say, "I've got you covered —come out with your hands up!"

Despite his sore throat, the boy called: "My God, Pop! You've killed the sheriff. Come out an' give up!"

At that moment the headlights of a car flashed on the highway. Smith, helpless without his gun, told young Pingley to flag the car for help, and then he ran over to cover in the shadow of the chimney outside the smaller section of the cabin. From there he saw that the automobile had passed on.

Once more Miller ordered Pingley to surrender. But the mountaineer remained menacingly silent in the darkness of the house. Miller cautiously stepped across the porch to the door. A former star athlete at the Handley High School, he was a crack shot and fearless.

He was within a foot of the door, plainly silhouetted against the pale moonlit sky, when suddenly the beseiged Pingley whacked the gun out of the officer's hand with the barrel of his shotgun. The revolver clattered to the floor.

In a bound, Miller hurdled the porch railing and crouched under the protective flooring. Carefully he stretched his hand up over the rim of the porch, feeling for his gun. For long seconds he fumbled, then his fingers gripped the cold steel.

Feeling secure now that he was armed and shielded from sight, he again commanded Pingley to surrender.

"I've got you covered, Pingley!" he said, slowly emerging into the open.

"You ain't got me — yet!" snarled Pingley.

There was a long second of intense silence.

Then—a flash and a roar as Pingley's shotgun blazed again. Miller uttered a cry of pain, and ran stumblingly, in a daze, across a small garden, and collapsed against a crude picket fence.

"Smitty! Smitty!" he called to his companion. "Get him!"

Smith leaped over a low retaining wall into the roadway and circled around to where Miller was lying unconscious, making a gurgling noise. Smith saw that he had been shot twice through the throat. Smith felt his faintly flickering pulse. He knew Miller was dying, and he was not sure whether Newcome was dead.

But he did realize that Pingley would shoot him, too, if he could. It would have been too dangerous to try and escape in the police car to get help. He set out on foot to give the alarm.

A MILE and a half down the pike he came upon a dark and desolate mountain cabin. Banging on the door, he waited breathlessly for some one to answer, resting after his long dog-trot run. Finally the door opened. Smith identified himself and asked for a gun.

The dour mountaineer — distrustful of the law, like all his ilk—was even more suspicious of Smith, because he had no uniform and could not show a badge.

"Ain't got no gun," said the hill-billy, slamming the door in Smith's face.

The officer pounded once more until the man opened the door slightly.

"Where can I get a gun?" he demanded.

"Try down the road a piece," the man replied dourly. "But I don't think they'll give you the loan of any firin' iron."

Smith half ran, half walked for two more miles. Once more he was refused.

"We ain't got no truck with the law here 'less we have to," the hillman said.

"But Pingley's shot Sheriff Newcome and State policeman Miller," insisted Smith. "I have to get help—I have to arrest Pingley!"

"Ain't none o' my business," the hill-billy declared. "But I'll tell you what I'll do—I'll drive you down to the turnpike, and you can tellyphone."

Smith climbed into the dilapidated auto of the old mountaineer. Carefully nursing his spluttering engine, the man eventually was able to reach an outpost of civilization in that rugged, wild country which is so amazingly unbelieveable to city people who live not far away. At the crossroads, Smith sent in an alarm to the police at Strasburg.

Quickly, the alarm was spread from Strasburg to the State police of Virginia and West Virginia, and to the county officers of Frederick and Shenandoah. Captain H. B. Nicholas, superintendent of the Virginia State troopers in that area, quickly set up a blockade around the almost inaccessible Great Mountain section in which Pingley lived. Trooper R. E. Bayliss, whom Newcome had first asked to accompany him, made a hurried trip to the convict camp near Gainsboro to secure bloodhounds.

By dawn the greatest manhunt in the history of Frederick County was under way. Lieut. J. A. Bingham of the State police, Trooper W. F. Hayden, Deputy Frank Pangle of Strasburg, in Shenandoah county, and Game Warden F. W. Pingley—no relation to the hunted killer—led separate groups of citizens into the desolate wooded area.

Other officers rushed to the Pingley cabin, where the mountaineer's wife, son and daughter were cowering in the upstairs bedroom.

The body of Sheriff Newcome was cold in death. Face up beside the corpse was the warrant that he had attempted to serve on his slayer. Miller was more dead than alive. He was rushed to the Winchester Memorial Hospital where it was found that the shot that had punctured his throat had pierced the bronchial tube, resulting in a deflated lung. A fraction of an inch below his right eye was a piece of metal that had barely missed blinding him. There was a shot through his hand.

An autopsy conducted by Coroner James A. Miller at Omp's Funeral home in Winchester revealed that the sheriff had died almost instantly from a murderous charge of gunshot in the back. The heavy slugs had entered between his eighth and ninth ribs, four inches from the spine, and had touched the lower lobes of the lungs and other vital organs.

THE bloodhounds were of little use. They had started off with a gleeful bay immediately after taking their clue from some of Pingley's clothing. But, as Pingley had tramped time after time over the rough and stony hills, his scent was everywhere. The dogs were baffled.

Lieut. Bingham, with Trooper Hayden, Deputy Pangle and Game Warden Pingley, were beating the tangled underbrush near Pingley's cabin while other members of the posse were scouring the mountainous country to the north and west, hoping to pick up a trail that might show whether the mountaineer had headed for West Virginia.

Quite unexpectedly, the little group came into a clearing, led there by the yapping of a collie dog.

"That's Pingley's mutt!" exclaimed the game warden.

"Then he must be around here somewhere!" said Hayden.

The collie pranced over to the game warden, leaping up at him in a friendly fashion, as though he were glad to see him.

"Where is he?" Pingley asked the dog. "Go get 'im!"

The collie frisked about and then headed through the brush.

The animal led the police to a clump of brushes. There, under a scrub tree, lay George Pingley, sound asleep.

Calling off the dog, lest it leap upon his master and awaken him, the officers approached their unsuspecting victim. Hayden noticed a heavy shotgun, cocked and ready to fire, lying beside the prostrate killer.

With his revolver at the ready, Hayden shouted: *"Pingley!"*

The sleeping man slowly raised his head, stirred uneasily, and then sat bolt upright when he saw the police surrounding him. He made a grab for his gun.

"Drop it!" commanded Bingham.

Realizing he was trapped, the man slowly raised his left hand, his right hand gradually moving toward the gun.

"Get your other hand up!" was the quick order.

"I'm a-comin'," he mumbled thickly, slowly raising his right hand over his head. "Don't shoot!"

Clumsily, the man managed to stagger to his feet and stumbled through the tall weeds toward the arresting officers. It was with difficulty that he prevented himself from falling flat on his face. He began to whimper.

Quickly, his hands were shackled.

The man swayed dizzily. The air around him reeked with the odor of potent mountain brew.

One of the officers held him up. "What's the matter with you?"

A hiccough was the reply. Then, looking back over his shoulder at an earthenware jug partly hidden in the grass, he licked his lips and said whiningly: "Gimme a 'nuther drink—"

Lieutenant Bingham stepped over to where Pingley had been lying and picked up the jug. It was almost empty.

"What a capacity he has!" he exclaimed.

"Ain't nawthin'," boasted Pingley, eyeing the jug thirstily. "Le'mme finish it."

"Nope! And from what I think is in store for you, Pingley, you've had your last drop of 'dew' on this earth! A warrant's out for you for murder!"

Pingley was blubbering like a baby when he was led down the mountainside. When a passable road was reached, a call was sent for a police car, and the mountaineer whisked away to jail.

"Takin' me to Winchester?" asked the sobering hillman.

"Not you! We wouldn't want to insult Mrs. Newcome by putting you under the same roof with her. After all, she lives in the Winchester jail as the sheriff's wife—er—widow."

News of the arrest of Pingley had spread quickly. Huge crowds gathered at the Winchester jail. They were disappointed when the prisoner was whisked through Winchester and taken to Woodstock, in Shenandoah county. At the Woodstock jail there was another crowd. Pingley was placed in a cell there, treated by a physician who gave him a sedative to fix up his hangover, and then rushed down the Valley Pike to Harrisonburg, in Rockingham county, about 75 miles from the scene of the slaying.

Commonwealth Attorney Burr P. Harrison of Frederick county asked the Grand Jury to indict Pingley for first degree murder. Action was immediate.

ALMOST two months to the day of the shooting in Mountain Falls, the giant mountaineer went on trial for his life before Judge Lemuel Smith and a jury of farmers in the historic Frederick County Circuit Court at Winchester.

Charles Curry, 80-year-old veteran lawyer who had handled more than 300 murder cases in his long career, defended Pingley. He charged that Sheriff Newcome "had sneaked into the house of George Pingley like a thief in the night and, after heaping indignities upon his wife and lovely young daughter, became engaged in a terriffic fight over a shotgun which ended in his death."

To refute this were Officer George Miller—miraculously recovered from his wounds—and Officer Edwin Smith, who dramatically recounted the events of the tragic night. Damaging testimony also was offered by young Harry Pingley, who had been held as a material witness, and the Sine brothers, mountaineer cronies of the sneering hillman, who testified concerning Pingley's hot-blooded hatred of the sheriff.

Pingley—clean-shaven and neat, in contrast to his first appearance when he was blubbering and shaking from alcohol—sat throughout the trial, fascinatingly interested. He was especially impressed when B. J. Parsons, ballistics expert of the Federal Bureau of Investigation, proved through microphotographs that it was Pingley's shotgun that had knocked the revolver from Miller's hand when he attempted to come to the aid of the mortally wounded sheriff.

On April 15—the fourth day

of the trial—a jury of farmers deliberated for 22 minutes and returned a verdict of guilty of murder in the first degree.

Stiffly erect, and with a dazed look on his face, Pingley stood up to hear Judge Smith solemnly intone:

"George W. Pingley, in accordance with the verdict of the jury, I sentence you to die by electrocution on the first day of July at the State penitentiary. God have mercy on your soul!"

Pingley was visibly shaken. He walked unsteadily back to his chair and sat down awkwardly. He fumbled with a copy of a newspaper which detailed the events of the trial on the day before, then clumsily tried to comfort his sobbing wife and daughter.

A few hours later he was taken by automobile to the Henrico county jail in Richmond. He spent most of the journey sucking oranges which had been given to him by hill-billy sympathizers.

WHAT'S IN A NAME?

AMONG the best known names of bogus noblemen is that of "Lord Beaverbrook," prince of heart-breakers. This highly-educated, middle-aged menace to women—and their bankrolls and jewelry—has, over a period of years, used more than 300 aliases and probably married hundreds of women, according to Deputy Police Commissioner Lyons, of New York City.

Some of the favorite pseudonyms used by "Lord Beaverbrook" are, Robert Whitman, Carl Rence, Arthur Brooks, Karl Edwards and Fred Stanley. According to police, his real name is Siegfried Sigamond.

Found guilty of swindling a Freeport, L. I., grandmother out of $90,000 in jewelry, he was sent to Sing Sing in 1929, to serve a five-to-ten year term.

"Lord Beaverbrook" was paroled from Clinton Prison last April, but his release was not generally made known. One month later he failed to report to parole officers.

Now, Federal authorities are looking for him to return him to Germany. He is wanted in several states and in Great Britain, France and Holland for alleged bigamous marries. But the spurious "Lord" has disappeared.

CLUE OF THE CROSS

By

Wallace King

THE Reverend Horace Broun mumbled a blessing, raised his bushy, white-thatched head and picked up the carving tools. For a moment, the Rev. Broun's twinkling, blue eyes rested on the two golden pheasants and the oven-browned potatoes swimming in a sea of gravy.

"A breast or a drumstick, Miss Finney?" he asked, poising the knife. There was no answer. Rev. Broun looked up expectantly, beaming on the little coterie of missionaries seated about the supper table, and for the first time noticed that the chair at the upper left-hand corner was empty.

"Why!" he said in surprise, "where is Miss Finney — I've never known her to be tardy to meals."

The four elderly spinsters seemed simultaneously to stare at the vacant chair, their lips pursed in an expression of disapproval. They did not like the young and vivacious girl who had but recently come out from Missouri to join the Methodist mission. She got overdue attention from the young converts. Besides, she seemed too

CHINA: *One of the oldest civilizations in the world uses modern methods in tracking down the murderers of a beautiful "foreign devil" and takes its vengeance with the cruelest execution known to mankind, "The Death of a Thousand Cuts".*

frivolous. To the elderly women, there was no place for laughter in the Lord's vineyard.

After a long moment, during which no one seemed willing to advance any excuse for the young missionary's absence, the Rev. Broun proceeded with the task of carving.

"Well, we shan't wait," he said briskly, adding with a laugh: "Frankly, I'm well nigh starved! What would you care for Miss Kiever . . . Miss Hebner . . . ?"

THEY ate in silence. The two house-boys and the serving maids slipped noiselessly about the carpeted room on thick velveted soles, pouring water, passing the buttered rolls and the vegetables. Only the clink of the silverware broke the heavy silence . . . that, and the dreary *tick-tock, tick-tock* of an antique clock, ceaselessly beating out time in a land where time is a meaningless eternity.

The little mission at Kingfowchu was nearly 1,000 miles inland from the sea. The town itself was unimportant and barely discernible even on the best maps of China. The great flotillas of *junks,* laden with precious cargos borne down through the western Yangtze River gorges, did not deign to stop at Kingfowchu, but sailed majestically on to bigger towns nearer the sea. Occasionally, pirate craft would drop anchor and the river devils would go on a spree of looting. But, except for these forages by the bandits, life was dull indeed.

True, Rev. Broun, some score or more years before, when he was young and strong and fired with a zealous passion to bring the light to the heathen, had tried to argue with the pirates, and persuade them that it was wrong to abduct the village maidens. But he had only been laughed at and had once been badly mauled for his troubles.

Finally, ridiculed by the townsmen in general, he prayed in solitude for the souls of these river devils, but did not go near them. He had, in fact, long ago lost patience with the pirates and besides, there was a lot of other work to do among the peasants in the rice paddies. During the past two years he had won over seven converts.

Thus, as the Rev. Horace Broun munched on his Sunday pheasant, careful not to bite into a stray buckshot in the tender meat, he was pleased as punch with himself—the thought of the seven converts warming the cockles of his heart.

"How about another helping, Miss Kiever - - -?" he asked.

Miss Kiever was about to decline, when the door leading into the kitchen was flung violently open, and Ah Sing, one of the six servants, came dashing into the dining room.

"Master! Master!" he called, wringing his hands.

"Don't you see we're dining?"

inquired the Rev. Broun, laying down his knife and fork and coldly eyeing the servant.

"But - - - master!" Ah Sing was visibly shaken, and there was a strange light in his eyes. "Missy Finney - - -"

"What about Miss Finney?" asked the missionary.

"Missy Finney - - - she dead!"

A gasp went up from the four women. Miss Hebner turned white, as though she was about to faint, and weakly reached for a glass of water.

"What!" shouted the Rev. Broun, half rising out of his chair.

"Missy Finney dead; all-same chop up with knife!" the servant exclaimed.

"Chopped up with a knife - - - oh!" and Miss McIvar, the eldest of the four women, slumped in her seat. "How perfectly terrible - - - how horrible!"

"Yes," said the servant.

"You mean, she's murdered - - - somebody killed her?" pressed the Rev. Broun.

"Maybe one - - - two - - - three people kill her," corroborated the servant, wildly gesturing. "Chop him up and take all Missy Finney's clothes."

"Where is she - - - where is the body?" asked the Rev. Broun.

"Out in rice paddy, outside village," said the servant.

"Well, get me my hat - - - quick!" Then, turning to the women, he said, "You girls better stay in here. It might possibly be river pirates roving about. Lock the windows and doors. I'll be back directly - - - "

WHEN the Rev. Broun reached the rice paddy where Ah Sing had reported the discovery of the young missionary's body, he had to force his way through the large crowd of stolid-faced peasants.

"Get out - - - get out of the way!" he panted, almost breathlessly, in the native dialect. "This is no concern of yours!"

Meekly the peasants drew back, making a path for the Rev. Broun. But as he strode to the spot where the body lay, the natives quickly closed in again, and stared . . stared at a nude, white corpse gazing with sightless eyes into the azure sky.

"I never saw a 'foreign devil' unclothed before," grinned a toothless farmer. "Ugh! The color of a dead fish!"

"Aiya," some one in the crowd laughed. Others joined in the merriment. For to the Chinese, death is not the awe-inspiring, sobering reality that it is to the Western mind; there are so many Chinese, and so many of them die! But the jabbering comments and the callous laughter infuriated the Rev. Broun.

After taking one horrified glance at the dead girl, the Rev. Broun whirled abruptly about and began belaboring the peasants with his umbrella—which was as much a part of his attire as his shoes and socks.

"Go away! Go away!" he shouted, almost hysterically. The crowd slowly stepped back, cringing as the swirling umbrella came dangerously close to their heads.

Just then a squad of soldiers in the army of a neighboring war-lord came upon the scene. A sergeant in charge, inquired into the trouble, and, being informed by the Rev. Broun that a young missionary had been murdered, he ordered his men to disperse the crowd. Grumbling, the peasants shuffled away from the scene—afraid of the soldiers, to whom they were always prone to looting forays, and equally angered at the white missionary who, as an alien, seemed to have so much power.

Left at last with his dead, the Rev. Broun kneeled in the damp earth and offered a prayer for Constance Finney who, just a scant three months before, had arrived in Kingfowchu to spread the Gospel.

The girl, only 22, and but recently out of college, had been placed in the care of the Rev. Broun. Her fine spirit and buoyant laugh indicated that she would make an ideal worker in the field. He had taken upon himself the task of teaching her the local dialect, and she had learned fast. Now his heart was leaden, there were ashes in his mouth.

As the missionary knelt on the brink of the rice paddy, unmindful that his knees had sunk deep into the soggy earth, a rough hand nudged him on the shoulder.

"It gets dark," said the sergeant. "Let us take the body into the village. Besides, it is indecent to leave it unclothed out in the cold of the dew - - - "

The Rev. Broun arose to his feet.

He looked down at the dead form, and all at once a wave of embarrassment swept over him - - - in the excitement of driving off the peasants and in the spiritual necessity for prayer he had not thought to cover the bare form from gaping, alien eyes. Quickly he removed his long, black coat and gently spread it over the girl's body.

"You are right," he agreed with the sergeant. "Let us carry her to the village."

When the soldiers had produced some long poles and the missionary, with the help of the sergeant, had placed the body across them, they picked up their grisly burden and marched unsteadily along the rough country road.

ARRIVING at the village, the body was taken to the mission and laid out on a black horse-hair sofa in the parlor. The town doctor, who had studied at a mission school on the seacoast, was summoned and arrived in the company of the chief magistrate and two local constables.

Dr. Li Ng, business-like in an immaculate white jacket, removed the Rev. Broun's coat from the corpse and stared at the frail body. Under the glare of the gasoline lantern—the mission was too far off the beaten track to boast of electric lights—it was plain to see that Constance Finney had not only been criminally assaulted and brutally murdered, but that she probably had been tortured to death!

The four spinsters, who had been fluttering about excitedly in the background, averted their eyes from the sight. Miss Havermeyer fainted dead away, and it was only after she had been restored to her senses that the Rev. Broun and the doctor could usher the four females into their own quarters.

"This is no place for you!" Rev. Broun thundered. "Go read your Bibles and pray for this poor, dear soul!"

Sniffling the women filed out of the parlour.

"This is a horrible thing, Reverend," muttered the doctor. "Look!"

The Rev. Broun mustered up his courage and looked. What he had taken for blood on the girl's hands was in reality her raw flesh—the skin had been peeled off from just below her elbow.

"They gave her 'The Gloves'," the doctor explained. "One of the most terrible tortures known —the hands were immersed in scalding water, boiled for a few minutes, and then the skin was peeled off, just like taking off a glove - - - "

The missionary shuddered. "But why? Why? Why should they do that to this harmless little girl - - - ?"

The doctor shrugged. "One never knows why anyone does anything," he replied. "And you know, Reverend that the people around here are among the most barbarous in the country - - - and look at her feet - - - "

The Rev. Broun stooped down and peered at the once shapely feet of the girl. They were badly scorched, and in one spot the flesh had been burned to the bone.

"They made her dance the 'Fire Dance,' too," the doctor added solemnly. "Some people get great pleasure out of watching a fellow being dancing nimbly on red-hot coals - - - now, look at her throat —see that tiny puncture there, where the windpipe is? That's what eventually killed her - - - they pierced her throat with a long, thin needle. The death that follows, they say, is very excruciating. . . . When did you last see this girl, Reverend?"

"Why, it must have been at lunch; no - - - it was during church services. I wasn't home for lunch - - - I went over to the Merchant Fan Lee's for a bite of luncheon."

"Well, she has not been dead for more than a few hours at most. Is there any way we can check back on her movements?"

"Why, yes; I'll call the ladies back in - - - they may be able to tell us something."

IN single file, the Misses Kiever, Hebner, Havermeyer and McIvar came gingerly into the room, darting a quick glance at the still form on the sofa, now modestly covered with a sheet. The Rev. Broun waved at them to be seated in four conveniently placed chairs in a far corner. The doctor, the magistrate, the Rev. Broun and the two constables drew up chairs and sat facing them.

"Now then," began the Rev. Broun, "can any of you ladies tell us when you last saw Miss Finney?"

The four women were strangely silent, darting meaningful looks at each other and then lowering their heads.

"Well - - - ?" prompted the Rev. Broun. "Surely one of you must have seen her after church."

The quartet remained close-mouthed. Then Miss Kiever, who had been nervously biting her lower lip, cleared her throat. Red-faced, she blurted out:

"I saw Miss Finney and - - - er - - - and young Fo Lin, the convert she made, outside the chapel after services. She - - - she didn't come back to the mission for lunch. Honestly how any respecting person can hobnob with a Chinese, even if he *is* a Christian, is beyond me - - - "

"Never mind your personal opinions, Miss Kiever," said Rev. Broun, rather harshly. "Let us know the facts, that's all. What happened then?"

"Well - - - Miss Finney and this Fo Lin person were chatting and laughing. I imagine Miss Finney was practicing her Chinese on him, and he was practicing his English lessons on her. Anyhow, they appeared much, much too frivolous, considering this is the Sabbath and all."

"Who is Fo Lin, may I ask?" inquired the chief magistrate. "I do not recall any family by that name in Kingfowchu."

"He is a recent convert to our faith," the Rev. Broun answered. "He came to us, ragged and hungry a week or so ago. We gave him sustenance for his body, clothes for his limbs and put hope in his soul! The change in him was amazing. He turned out to be a very splendid young man!"

"Did I hear you say he talked the English tongue?"

"Yes; he speaks it a little."

"Did he, by any chance, tell you where he came from?"

"No."

"Perhaps, Reverend, you have been harboring a reptile," put in

Dr. Li Ng. "A 'Rice Christian,' so to speak - - - one who is easily converted spiritually for the sake of material gains alone - - - I know too many of my countrymen, more's the pity, who pretend to worship your God because of the food and the rice you woo them with - - - but inside their hearts they worship their own gods and dragons - - - "

"You are a little cynical, Doctor," remarked the Rev. Broun soothingly. "But what we are here for now is to solve a fiendish crime, not to discuss religion."

"Very true. You may proceed, Miss Kiever."

"Well, when I turned into the mission house gate, I saw Miss Finney and this Fo Lin strolling away, chatting with each other. She must have gone off with him—that's all I can say! Except for this: that Miss Finney is a disgrace to all of us and who can say but that perhaps she deserves - - - "

"Miss Kiever!" shouted the Rev. Broun.

The spinster sniffled into a 'kerchief. "I'm sorry," she said. "I didn't really mean to say that."

"Humpf!" commented the Rev. Broun. Then, "If none of you have anything to add to what Miss Kiever has told us, you are excused."

The four ladies arose and stiffly marched out of the room.

WHILE the two constables were sent to gather all information concerning Fo Lin; the chief magistrate, the doctor and the missionary held a council of war.

"Our best clue, of course, is your new convert," said the magistrate. "If we can find him, we'll make him speak even if we have to grind him slowly to pieces in an exquisite little device known as 'The Bone Crusher.' Next, we must locate Miss Finney's clothes, for surely they must have been disposed of in some thieves' bazaar. Do you know whether she had any money with her?"

"Money?" The Rev. Broun raised his eyebrows in skepticism. "If she had any - - - and no missionary has, you know - - - she put it in the collection plate."

"Did she wear any jewelry?" inquired the doctor.

"I think she always wore a small gold cross on a chain about her neck - - - but it wouldn't be valuable enough to commit a murder over - - - worth three or four dollars at the most, I'd say."

The doctor got up and went over to the still form on the couch. He lifted a corner of the sheet, stared intently for a second, then covered again the pain-wracked face of the dead girl.

"No cross there now," he said in a flat tone.

At that moment, one of the constables banged on the solid mission house door with the butt of his gun. The Rev. Broun hurried across the room and let him in.

"Big news! Big news!" shouted the constable, breathing hard after an apparently long run.

"Did you find him?" asked the magistrate. "Quick, tell us!"

"No - - - but we found out who Fo Lin is! He's the leader of a pirate boat that has been coasting up and down the Yangtze, pillaging and kidnaping. Only a few minutes ago, word was received that the pirates had attacked a Catholic mission about 20 miles up the river, and slain all the people!"

"No!" exclaimed the Rev. Broun, rising excitedly from his chair.

"When did this happen?" asked the magistrate.

"Yesterday."

"Then, perhaps, they are moving eastward, toward the sea," put in the doctor. "Has an alarm been sent to the towns and villages to watch out for them?"

"Yes."

"Good!" said the magistrate. "If vigilance is kept, they can't escape. Their heads will be stuck on sharpened stakes rising out of the river bottom as a warning to the rest of their breed - - - "

"A lot of good that does!" grumbled the doctor. "Last year there were nearly 50 heads on exhibit right on the banks of this town - - - and did the pirates pay any heed? No! They came in and burned and looted and stole more than a dozen of the prettiest girls in Kingfuchow!"

"Ah!" said the magistrate, with a wry smile. "You don't realize that if we can get 50 heads a year, the pirates will soon disappear - - -"

The young doctor scowled at the magistrate, then deliberately arose from his chair. "Well - - - I guess we've done everything we can, Reverend. If you like, I'll wire to Hankow for a coffin - - - "

"Thank you, doctor. I'll go with you; I must cable the poor child's parents." Turning to the magistrate, he asked, "Do you suppose we can signal a river steamer to stop at Kingfuchow? It would be simpler to take the body by boat than to try and reach a railroad."

"That will be done, Reverend," the magistrate said. "And, in parting, allow me to extend my sympathies to you and the other missionaries. Meanwhile, I will have every available man search out this pirate, Fo Lin. Perhaps, when Nanking gets the report of the murder, your Government will send an American warship after them, too. I am sorry my country is so unsafe for you Americans in the interior. Some day, we hope to be rid of pirates and bandits - - - "

IT was mid-July, 1937. A hot sun beat down upon the narrow, reeking streets of Hangkow.

Coolies—the beasts of burden of China—were scarcely able to haul their awkward, heavy-laden carts of merchandise; rickshaw coolies could no more than dog-trot with their impatient passengers through the narrow streets.

The city—later to become the provisional capital of China before the onslaught of the Japanese war machine—drowsed. Even the *wonks*—the mongrel dogs that scavenge in every Chinese city—were too disinterested to hunt for food, too exhausted, even, to shake off the buzzing flies that nestled on their skinny, mangy bodies.

But not even the heat deterred the Chinese police—much. The murderous onslaught of the river pirates at the Catholic and Methodist missions had brought stern warnings from Nanking, the capital, that the killers must be apprehended at all costs—foreign governments were putting on pressure. That meant warboats, concessions, huge indemnities - - - all loathesome to China which through the years has hardly been able to call its country its own: for every slaying of a missionary meant further inroads of the Western Powers.

"They should keep these foreign preachers out," said Detective Ah Leong, wiping his perspiring brow with a huge cotton 'kerchief. "They always bring trouble . . . "

"Ai!" replied his partner, Choy Sing. "Trouble and gunboats!"

The two men, finding it too hot to talk, walked slowly toward the riverfront, stepping over sleeping dogs, walking around children listlessly playing in the street, and envying the shopkeepers, drowsing in the doorways.

They had proceeded to within a short distance of the river when Choy Sing suddenly stopped short. "Look here," he said. "It might be cooler down on the banks of the Yangtze, but do you seriously think we'll find Fo Lin's pirate craft tied up there? If he's in this area, he's tied his ship upriver somewhere and he and his men have walked into town. He's not going to be so stupid as to steer his vessel right under our noses, for surely he must know that there is a price on his head - - - "

"There is truth in what you say," remarked Ah Leong. "But my idea of going down to the river - - - outside, of course, expecting to get a cooling breeze - - - was to inquire if any of the boatmen had seen the pirate craft. We have a good description of it, sent from upriver, and it was headed toward Hankow."

"Even so, he'd still not dare to moor his boat among the trading junks!"

"A wise thought, I will admit," said Ah Leong. "Have you any further suggestions, though?"

Choy Sing wrinkled his brow, deep in thought. One of the most astute of the Hangkow constabulary, he had a reputation for ferreting out the more crafty criminals.

"Yes," he finally replied. "The Thieve's Market - - - it won't be as cool as the river, and it will be odiferous, but - - - "

"But what?"

"You know from the report of the murder from Kingfowchu, the Young Lily (a term for a pretty girl) was robbed not only of her clothes but her jewlery as well. A gold cross." Choy Sing extracted a crumpled bit of white rice paper from his pocket and studied the chicken-scratch ideographs. "Yes," he said, reading the list. "A gold cross; a leather purse; a blue silk dress; patent leather slippers (how can they manage to wear those things?) and various undergarments - - - all silk."

"So - - - ?"

"So we'll visit the Thieves' Market! None of the women folk in the pirate band would have need for the foreign garments. Fo Lin would sell them. And the cross would bring many dollars —if it was good gold. We'll try the market!"

"Excellent," sighed Ah Leong. Too many times had he had to visit the Thieves' Market, an institution famous in every Chinese city where pilfering servants "ransom" their master's goods and where marauding bandits and pirates get quick cash for their loot from ransacked villages and scuttled cargo junks. Trying to locate stolen property there was a long and tedious task, especially when the stall proprietors recognized prospective customers as police, and hid whatever goods they thought they might be searching for.

The two detectives turned down a narrow winding side street and headed toward the market place. Once there, they found it a bedlam. Even if the rest of Hangkow was snoozing in the shade, there were always robbery victims trying to buy back their own precious goods, and scores of people on the lookout for bargains in the way of precious jades, hi-jacked bolts of fine silks and other valuable objects that could be picked up for a song.

THE task of Ah Leong and Choy Sing was not an easy one. In every other country there are pawn shops where goods are carefully recorded, the books open to police inspection: a tiny clue in a pawnshop often has led to the solving of many of the world's most atrocious crimes. But no books were kept in the Thieves' Market. One simply had to look closely, ferret out objects from beneath piles of assorted articles and - - - more often - - - ask the stallkeeper for exactly what had been stolen. The marketman, in turn, could produce the article, if he had it, or swear that he had never seen such goods - - -

it all depended on how he judged the customer and what he thought he could extort from his purse.

The two detectives slowly walked from stall to stall, eyeing the merchandise. The market was divided into separate sections, one for clothing, another for silks, a third for jewelry, and so on.

"The gold cross is our best clue," remarked Ah Leong, after casting a discouraged eye over some foreign frocks hanging in one of the stalls. "These dresses all look the same to me - - - "

The pair drifted over toward the jewelry stalls. Precious stones, cool jades and gleaming gold were scattered in profusion on the tables. Carefully examining a trayful of golden baubles, Sing Choy picked up a gold cross - - - then another - - - and another!

"The market's full of these things!" he snorted.

But Ah Leong's eyes glistened.

"Yes! That must be loot from the Catholic mission beyond Kingfowchu - - - Fo Lin and his band have disposed of their loot here!"

"Was there any sort of identification on the cross belonging to the Young Lily?" asked Ah Leong, carefully examining half a dozen gold crosses he held in his hand.

Choy Sing once more pulled out the rice paper with its notations, and studied it. "It would seem that the cross was engraved with foreign characters on the reverse." He described the initials "C" and "F." "They are possibly some symbol which is beyond my ignorance," he said. "But watch for such curious markings."

Choy Sing asked the marketman if he had more gold crosses.

Smiling toothlessly, the man shook his head. "Got too many now," he mumbled. "And no one seems to come and claim them!"

Ah Leong and Choy Sing wandered to the next shop. There they found five more gold crosses, some of them ornate, but none with the mystic "C. F." on the back. Still more crosses were found in other shops. Finally, Ah Leong let out an exclamation. "Here it is!" he said.

Immediately the stall-keeper was placed under technical arrest and hurried to the Municipal court for questioning.

"Have mercy! I am innocent!" he kept repeating as he was hustled through the streets.

In the police station he was taken into a room which boasted but a table and two carved teakwood chairs. Along the walls, however, were knouts and strange iron contraptions for torture—"boots" that crushed the bones of the feet; tongs that yanked fingernails out by the roots; gimlets, like screwdrivers, which bored out the eyes; and a dozen other devices calculated to make a man talk— for the Chinese have been experts at torture from time immemorial.

The frightened marketman, his

hands bound behind his back, stood facing the detectives and half a dozen other officers as the chief constable and the magistrate lolled in the chairs, drumming the table with their long fingernails.

"Where did you get this cross?" asked Ah Leong.

"I bought it."

"From whom?"

"A man."

One of the attendants, at a nod from the chief constable, ripped off the stall-keeper's blue cotton shirt, took a five-rope leash from the wall and swung it mightily. The ends of each leash were weighted with lead, and as the ropes viciously encircled the man's nude torso, the leaden weights sounded dully, and knocked the wind out of the man.

"Now - - - will you speak! 'A man' sold it to you! We know that - - - ! What did he look like? How much did you give him? Quick!"

His face contracted with pain, the marketman gasped out what he knew. His description fitted that of the pirate, Fo Lin.

"Have you ever seen this man before?"

"Yes, honorables - - - many times!"

"Does he live in Hangkow?"

"No; but he comes frequently to Hangkow from somewhere up the Yangtze. But - - - O! Your Honors! he will slice me into a million pieces if he knows I told you this! - - - he stays at the Inn of the Weeping Willow when he comes to Hangkow."

The detectives looked at each other knowingly. The Inn of the Weeping Willow was a notorious waterfront dive, a hangout of gamblers and dope fiends, where the sing-song girls made the nights hideous with bawdy songs, raucous laughter and — often — tortured screams.

"Is Fo Lin there now?" asked the magistrate. "Be truthful!"

"Yes, Honorable - - - if he has not already gone back up the river."

THE man was held in the police station as Ah Leong and Choy Sing went to investigate the inn. Changing into tattered clothes, and smearing their faces and garments with a red stain to resemble blood, they posed as members of Fo Lin's pirate crew. To make it look real, Ah Leong made as if to support Choy Sing, who simulated a weakened and wounded condition. Knocking loudly on the door, Ah Leong switched from the Hangkow dialect to an upriver speech as a wizened old crone peered at him through a peep-hole.

"Quick!" said Ah Leong. "Is Fo Lin here? It is a matter of life and death - - - we have just escaped the police, and my companion here is badly hurt!"

"Yes - - - Fo Lin is here. But he cannot be disturbed. He is full of wine and can appreciate no one but girls!"

"But you must let us in! We must warn him, so that he can escape - - - even now the police may be trailing us to your door. You don't want the Inn of the Weeping Willow wrecked, do you?"

"No! No!" muttered the old woman, unlatching the door. "Come in, but stay quiet. Fo Lin will be out of his stupor shortly - - - my! what a drinker. Seven bottles of strong Dragon Blood liquor, almost at a gulp!"

When the two detectives were admitted, a cordon of police who had been watching the inn, closed in slowly and cautiously, for it had been arranged that, if the detectives were permitted to enter, it would be a signal that the pirate chieftain was inside. At a sign from the leader, the police rushed the inn, some attacking the front door, while others broke in through the back.

Inside, Ah Leong and Choy Sing whipped out revolvers and cowed the inn-keeper and a small of group of gamblers engrossed in a game of *fan tan*.

"Fo Lin - - - where is he?" snapped Ah Leong.

Cringing, the old crone who had opened the door, pointed upstairs. "There," she whispered. "In the Room of a Million Delights . . . the one overlooking the river."

Ah Leong bounded up the stairs while his companion stood guard below. Reaching the indicated room, Ah Leong put his shoulder to the door and shoved. It splintered under the impact, and Fo Lin, the pirate, was so taken by surprise at the sudden entrance, that he could only stare groggily through blood-shot eyes.

As a matter of fact, the bloodthirsty pirate was at considerable disadvantage, for not only was he not clothed, but he was manhandling a Chinese fiddle, much to the amusement of a giggling singsong girl - - - and with the fiddle in his clumsy hands, he was unable to make a quick snatch for his gun.

"All right, Fo Lin! The fun's over!" said Ah Leong. "Get dressed and come along!"

Meekly, the pirate donned his clothes—the very garments that had been given to him by Constance Finney at the mission.

AT the police station, Fo Lin was far from the blustering cutthroat who had terrified whole provinces, towns and villages for a 500 mile stretch up and down the Yangtze. Questioned in the room equipped with all its instruments of torture, the pirate was no longer the tiger, but a lamb. As his eyes darted from one pain-wracking device to the other, he winced: for such is the manner of bullies—they can give with glee, but they cannot bear to suffer themselves.

"Why did you kill the Young Lily?" asked the magistrate.

"Because I loved her," blandly

replied Fo Lin. "But she did not love me."

"Love! What do you know about love?" asked the Magistrate scornfully.

"I know as much as the next man," staunchly replied the pirate.

"For that - - - five lashes from the knout," ordered the magistrate.

Fo Lin howled and begged for mercy as the thongs swirled through the air and clung painfully to his ribs.

After that ordeal was over, the magistrate leaned forward, resting his elbows on the table, and remarked quietly: "Now, Fo Lin, begin at the beginning - - - and remember, for every lie your soul will sizzle a thousand, thousand years in the pits of the Fire Demon. Proceed!"

Fo Lin wet his lips and began:

"We heard that there was much gold in the Catholic mission. We sent a few men up there to pose as mendicants and spy around. The men were fed and preached to - - - and saw gold candlesticks and other objects about. They reported that there was sufficient gold to make us all rich. But when we raided the place that night, the priests put up a battle. We had to kill three of them. And then what we had thought was gold turned out to be brass!

"We had lost two men in the fight ourselves, and my men demanded vengeance, first, for being fooled into thinking the articles were gold, and second, because of the death of our comrades. The priests had been subdued and bound. We had promised not to harm them but some of the more hot-headed members of our party voted to slay them then and there. I speak the truth when I say I pleaded with them not to . . . that the bodies would be quickly found and we would be hunted down by the warboats of the foreign devils. So, we led them down to the river bank - - - and there, in the peaceful cool of the river breeze, and with the singing of birds to gladden their ears, we mercifully drowned them."

"How many were there?"

"Seven," answered the pirate. "And had it not been for a treacherous tide that washed up the bodies, no one would have been the wiser, for it would have been thought that they had deserted their place of prayer while their bodies would float to the sea, to vanish forever. But even the most wily plans can go askew, as you can see - - - "

"Well, what about the murder of the girl?"

"That, O Honorable! is a different story. I went to the mission to see if by any chance there might be something worthwhile - - - for, as you know, the warlords have combed the provinces with a fine comb lately, leaving little for a self-respecting river man to live on. At the mission I saw the Young

Lily. She was beautiful, just like the talking shadows (movies) that you can see right here in Hangkow.

"Strangely, she took compassion upon me. She gave me rice and some fowl, regarded my old and ragged clothes and gave me these, that I am wearing. She talked softly, and I was enthralled by her voice. I could not hear eonugh from her cherry petal lips. She talked to me of a strange god, and I listened to that, too. She asked me if I would renounce my own gods and accept her god. I said I would - - - only to hear her talk, to look into her strange, blue eyes, to regard her hair that was like gold. I loitered in Kingfuchow.

"Then, on the day of the foreigners' worship, the Young Lily took me into the house of prayer. Afterward, I asked her to walk down to the river bank to listen to the orioles that nest in the willows. She agreed to go with me. And on that walk I determined to make her mine - - - we reached the river and my men hailed me. I said to the girl: 'These are friends of mine. Let us visit them on their boat.' Innocently, she accepted. I took her into the cabin, and without her knowing it, the others untied the mooring ropes and we drifted away on the tide - - - "

FO LIN stopped, the perspiration now standing out on his brow. He seemed to be living over again that fatal Sunday.

"Go on," said the magistrate.

"When the Young Lily realized that she was aboard a moving boat, she started to scream. I clasped my hand over her mouth and threw her down on the floor. 'You are mine!' I said.

"She kicked and scratched and tried to fight free. I had two of the men tie her legs and arms. We stuffed a cloth in her mouth, so that she could give no outcry until we had passed safely past the village. Then I told her that she must first tell me where all the gold was that the mission had - - - for we knew there must gold, for how else could the missions spend so much? She only shook her head.

"One of my assistants said that he would make her speak, and produced a charcoal brazier, on which we cooked our rice. Taking off the girl's shoes, he placed her foot into the red-hot coals, slowly at first. But she only fainted. After a while we placed her other foot in the fire, but still she remained stubborn - - - and went into a state of unconsciousness."

It was then, Fo Lin explained, that the girl was assaulted.

"When she revived, the Young Lily was more dead than alive. Surely, we thought, she would now tell us where the mission gold was hidden. Still she was silent. Then, we remembered that 'The Gloves' was a never-failing method of making a person speak. We boiled water and tied a string tightly around her arm, just below the elbow. Then we plunged her hand into the water, right up to the string, and held it there. In a few minutes, we peeled off the skin. When she refused to talk we did the same to the right hand.

"Perhaps it was fear and pain that made her speechless, but we did not think of that then - - - anyway, we decided that she would be useless without her hands - - - the exposure of the flesh to the air gradually is fatal, you understand, for a person can touch nothing with them, and starves if nothing else. We decided to put her out of misery - - - and skewered her wind-pipe.

"We could have used a sword, but that was too quick for most of the men, who really relish such a circus as we had that day - - - she was still alive when we put back into shore near the village and left her body in the rice paddy.

"All the gold we got, in both raids, was the Young Lily's little cross - - - it brought but a trifling sum from the thieving marketmen. You know the rest, O! Honorable! Have mercy on one who has, at least, rid the country of a few treacherous foreign devils - - - "

The magistrate looked at Fo Lin in mild amazement. The callous recital of the horrible murder of the seven priests and the girl and then the brazen plea for mercy left him speechless.

Finally, he cleared his throat.

"It is true, as you have said, that you have rid the country of a few foreigners whom you despise, but it is also true that this country must guarantee if it can, the safety of these foolish people who insist on residing outside the treaty ports. These killings are damaging to China, for each one costs us money, land and prestige. Therefore, I must sentence you, Fo Lin, and all your men, to die."

Fo Lin hung his head as he heard the magistrate speak. Then he was led out into the courtyard of the *yamen*. There his 13 followers already were on their knees, in a sort of semi-circle, their hands bound behind them. All were naked to the waist. Fo Lin was placed facing his men. Then began one of the cruelest executions known to man—"The Death of a Thousand Cuts."

First one man and then the others were slowly sliced to pieces —an ear, a finger, an arm was lopped off - - - And as the swordsmen went about their butchery, every one of the doomed men was forced to watch the sufferings and agonies of his companions.

Fo Lin was the last to die.

Thus China—the oldest civilization in the world—avenged the murder of a lovely "foreign devil" from a distant, barbarous land.

CARNAGE IN CAIRO

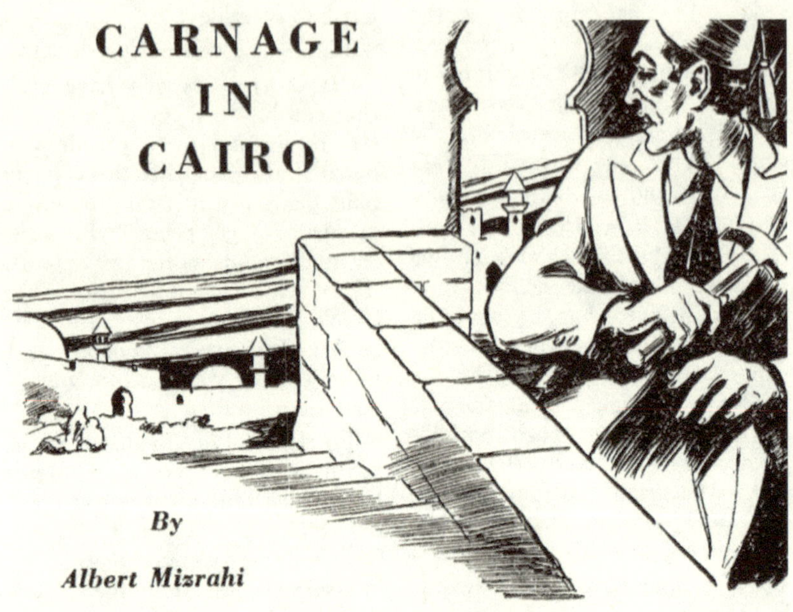

By

Albert Mizrahi

THE neighborhood woke dully to a cry in the night; then sharply roused, as shriek after shriek of a woman in mortal terror, died suddenly on the air.

Over Cairo sparkled a crust of stars, from horizon to horizon, like a rug of diamonds spread there by a geni's lavish whim. Only a few moments earlier, all the city lay tranquil beneath the flickering heavens, sleeping in the dark shadows of its own sprawling streets. Within-doors was darker still; for it lacked only twenty minutes to midnight. And in this intense indoor murk slunk the yet blacker substance of a prowler.

This sinister shade produced a pass-key. The outer hall door yielded to it quietly. Safely in, the figure froze: tensely listened to the rhythmic breathing of deep slum

EGYPT: *"Allah knows what is best for you when you yourselves do not," says the Koran. Yet, when the evil tongues of gossips took possession of Fahmy's soul, five innocent people met a horrible death.*

ber. Satisfied, the shadow glided on as silently as Death, through the parlor where two persons slept, straight for a lone figure in an adjacent chamber. Stealthily the phantom drew a heavy object from beneath its clothing, and held this ready as a weapon.

Reaching the bed, the spectre paused to mark a fatal spot—raised the weapon—and without sound or tremor crushed the sleeper's skull with one expert blow. Following the muffled thud, the silence was intense.

Turning, then, the killer-shadow coolly quit the room. But out in the parlor it paused reflectively and as an afterthought singled out the lighter sleeper of the two there: this one's breath came less deeply, less convincingly. As the monster bent to inspect the sleeper's face, the latter stirred and a man's voice grunted quizzically from the bed. In a flash the hovering figure cracked the weapon down with such precision that no outcry or noise escaped.

Only one breathed now in the room where two had slept a moment before. The demoniac shade moved towards this second sleeper: again bending curiously as though to identify the person, again casting a pall over the slumberer's rest. This time as the sleeper stirred, the demon hesitated as it poised the weapon aloft to strike; then, abruptly deciding, ferociously dealt the blow. The victim rattled in his throat, and the room was next plunged in eerie silence. Slowly, the visitor turned about to face the closed door to still another room. With less assurance, now, it slid to the door, opened, paused cautiously a moment before entering.

Two half-grown figures lay in one bed, and on a nearby bunk was another. The pair slept soundly; but not so the other.

"Who's there?" came a girl's peremptory voice from the bunk. The breath of the sleeping pair put an edge on the dead, answering silence. "What's that!" persisted the girl, still startled. Nothing stirred save the uninterrupted even breathing of the small two-some in their bed.

Not until the alert girl, lulled out of her nervous fancy, tossed herself into comfortable position for sleep again, did the roving shadow detach itself from the dark wall. Bludgeon upraised for instant business, it meant no mercy as it made for the wakeful girl. Within striking range, the weapon came fiercely down. But at that instant the girl shifted her position, and the blow only grazed her head.

Again the weapon struck, but missed a fatal spot as the intended victim, bounding up with a shrill cry, fell unconscious to the floor under the second impact. The smaller two in their big bed, awakened, began a clamor which they quickly ceased in favor of the better strategy of hiding: one under the covers, the other all the way under the bed. A crunch ended the one as coldbloodedly as the extinction of a roach.

In the search and scuffle after the other, the battered girl upon the floor had time to recover consciousness and an opportunity to drag herself to the open window. Shrieking for help, she heard her other room-companion bashed to death. To escape the killer who turned again upon her, she jumped out the window to the court below. Silence fell again.

The triumphant fiend cast about for an escape; the open window seemed the best and swiftest. Through it he fled into the open black of the star-lit court.

TRANQUIL Nag-Hamadi village is three days' distance by *felucca* up the Nile from Cairo. There, Ez-Zed Gohar, a laborer, had gathered his family about him, as he fearfully yet wearily awaited his end. For five wasting years he had put up a struggle against a malady whose nature the doctors could not diagnose. Two thousand years of Egyptian medicine and Arab science to draw upon, and all they could do was to probe, prescribe—and hope! But towards his end, the long-suffering man was so filled with the certainty that his last hours were running out, that those about him knew he must be right. It was not long after they had all assembled, that his life began ebbing swiftly. He received their tears, blessed them each in turn, and passed over The Bridge to the eternal delights of paradise.

Laila, his faithful wife, though submissive to irrevocable Fate, could not restrain her tears; they rolled in streams down her cheeks. Around her, scared and loudly sobbing, hung her three daughters; poor Nefissa taxed the maturity of her sixteen years to give comforting support to her eleven year old sister Fahima; and Aziza, though only twelve, clasped her mother's hand almost understandingly. Fahmy, the son of the house, stood opposite, by his father's cold right hand; he was stunned and silent.

An *ulema* read from the Koran, and offered consolation.

"In the Book of Imran it is written: 'A man does not die save by the will of Allah; his term of days is fixed'," said the learned man. "The departed was a good, alms-giving man; do not now begrudge him his reward. 'He who sets his desire upon the blessings of eternal life, shall be vouchsafed that'."

"Bismillah elrohman elrahim!" the mourning family murmured. "In the name of clement and merciful Allah."

The *ulema* left. The mournful bustle of preparations for the final rites got under way. Laila moved as in a fever; yet she somehow managed through it all, keeping up routine—so vital in bolstering a stricken household's morale. She had time to notice, too, how young Fahmy drooped; that worried her.

She was not his mother, but she had a mother's affection for him; and her heart went out to him. Ez-Zed Gohar's first wife was Fahmy's true mother; she had died at Fahmy's birth.

Laila was Ez-Zed Gohar's second wife: she was the only mother Fahmy had ever known, of course. As was perhaps only natural, though, the ties of affection between Ez-Zed and Fahmy had always been especially strong. In his twenty years growing, Fahmy had turned more and more to his father for understanding and encouragement. If she had ever unwittingly failed in a mother's affection or duty to him before, Laila tried hard to help her step-son now in his grief.

Life's routine, and work especially, is a powerful antidote for moping. Laila kept the family to its routine. Through her servant, Mohamed, she sent word to Fahmy's employer, who was a life-long friend of Ez-Zed Gohar's, to keep the boy busy.

SOME days after the final rites, the atmosphere in the household began to lighten a little. Swept along by day-to-day problems, the children ceased their weeping. And Fahmy centered all his energies on his cabinet-making. Life resumed its even flow. For the first time, Laila began to realize what strain she had been under for the past five years: scrimping to pay the doctors, pinching to buy drugs at the apothecary's, keeping the household going, nursing Ez-Zed, minding the children in their progressive phases year in and year out, keeping them all fed and clothed. Now that it was all over, she was ready to fly to pieces in nervous exhaustion. But she pulled through: the girls still depended on her, and no less did Fahmy.

Within a comparatively short time, the sad shadow in Fahmy's countenance gave place to a well-known dreaminess; and the family perked up. Nefissa saw it first, and whispered it to Aziza: both were enthralled, but Fahima was not so ripe for romantic sympathies. It was from her that Laila learned of Fahmy's supposed love-dream. She watched the boy, and, sure enough: there was that look in his eye.

"Perhaps you had better see how the land lies at the shop," she bade Mohamed, with a housekeeper's practical sense.

"He is forging ahead," Mohamed reported when he had looked into things. He elaborated: business was good; and Fahmy was being entrusted with work on more valuable pieces of furniture than he would, in quieter times, have been allowed to touch. He was making good; and his future was green! Laila was pleased and relieved. "I heard some mention there at his shop, of a Zenaib: our neighbor's daughter, I suppose. They were chaffing the young master about her."

"She is just the kind of girl I should wish him to have an eye upon: beautiful, and strong!" exclaimed Laila happily. "Not a word of this, though: Fahmy might misunderstand."

"Not a word, mistress, of course!" vowed Mohamed. "I understand."

Laila had a new thought to worry her now. Should she stay or go, under the circumstances? By staying, she could run Fahmy's affairs more economically than anyone else. But by leaving the way clear for her step-son to bring a wife home, she might please him even more. She had resources of her own; so that did not enter into the problem. What she had was not a great deal; but enough to keep herself and the children: it consisted mainly of her own dower-possessions, since Ez-Zed's doctors had left very little of his life's savings. But there was more to life than being merely independent: what would best serve Fahmy? She saw that the only one who could answer that was Fahmy himself; and she decided to ask him at the first opportunity.

That same evening, when Fahmy put in his appearance for supper, he was very dispirited. At once, Laila's conscience bit her: no doubt Fahmy had learned somehow of Mohamed's errand over at his shop. She put in an uncomfortable evening waiting for him to tax her with spying. She could explain, if he gave her a chance; but no opening came. She let the matter go, of whether she should move or not, until another time. She did not wish to trouble him. For perhaps, after all, the boy had some other problem on his mind. Perhaps he was troubled, as was more than probable, about the means of scraping together the first down payment on Zenaib's dowery. Laila, at thought of it, wished she could afford to let him have the money his father had left; but he was young and a man and could earn all he needed, while she could not: she had to keep her capital together!

Neither her probe into his affairs, nor worry over raising Zenaib's dowery-payment, had anything to do with Fahmy's mood. This certainty flashed upon Laila's mind the next morning when, stopping to examine some goods at a village shop, she found there ahead of her a certain curdled dame who once had snared for Ez-Zed Gohar at about the time Laila had found favor in his eyes.

"Bless you! It's nice to see you so well and prosperous," this neighbor nodded, smiling thinly. "Your step-son mentioned only last night how you had entirely recovered from your sorrow."

"Oh yes," sparred Laila coolly.

"Poor boy; he has such burdens now for one so young. Ah well; he's getting older, though, every day, isn't he!—He wants to take a wife, I hear," added the sharp one, pityingly.

"He does; but he has already made his choice," retorted Laila. Her neighbor reddened at the shot; and Laila knew that she had converted an ill-wisher into an active enemy. She knew, too, that compared to the fang of such a hater, that of the asp was as harmless as the bite of an earthworm. But, still warm with indignation at the other's sly insinuations, she little cared how her neighbor felt.

Belatedly, Laila realized that her newly made enemy, in other days while stalking Ez-Zed Gohar, had cultivated Fahmy; she had kept it up, and still had the unwary youth duped. Talking with her last night, Fahmy must have received some of the woman's mischievous shafts; and that undoubtedly was what accounted for his glum manner. Laila was as clear about that as if she had personally witnessed everything. Seeing through it now, she knew she should expect to hear more than ever of such slanderous inuendos, in retaliation for her provocative retort. She was right; nor was it long before her fears commenced materializing.

LAILA was in the village soon thereafter, and started for home later than she had planned. As happens at such times, everything conspired to hold her up. At one intersection, a long strung-out camel-pack cut across in front of her, leisurely led and smugly following: that delayed her several minutes. She lost five minutes when a mild little donkey straining under his mountainous load, suddenly lay down in the middle of the street and died: the crowd which gathered at the donkey-owner's wails and curses, filled the narrow street from side to side and blocked all passage.

To make up for these delays, she stepped as quickly as she knew how, taking every short-cut there was. The last of these short-cuts was a back lane not far from home. As she hurried along it, a hail ahead brought her up in surprise.

"Why, Allah bless you: are you not the son of the lamented Ez-Zed Gohar?" shrilled the voice. It was that of a notorious neighborhood gossip; and she seemed to care little how far her words carried. Laila heard Fahmy acknowledge the identity. "Aye; I've seen you coming and going!—And your father before you. He was an upright man, he was: oh, how young he was, to pass away! Who would have thought of him as ripening for a natural death at that age: not I!"

Fahmy tried to break away. Laila raged powerlessly at the cruel torment these harpies put the boy to! She could have wept; but, instead, swallowed her fury in attentive silence. "Your mother must have been distracted with grief over such a loss," said the tongue-wagger; and Laila waited now for the harridan to get to the point at last. "She was a step-mother, though, wasn't she. Yes; now I recollect. We all thought your own mother so beautiful; so warm hearted and sweet and helpful! She was such an affectionate clinging type, too! It was a strange match your father made when he married a second wife as independent as your step-mother!—Well; so now she's free again!—So it is: most of us would find such freedom empty; but I imagine she is fortunate enough to find comfort in it. And, since Fate has decreed it, why shouldn't she be philosophical, after all!"

"Woman!—Excuse me," choked Fahmy, distinctly enough for Laila to catch his words and triumph at his proper indignation.

"Allah go with thee, poor young man," called the woman after him.

Laila turned about and went back by the long way home. She was glad of this incident, though. It would innoculate and harden Fahmy against the slanders and inuendos which were evidently rife just now. Later, the poisonous source would dry up; and they could all breathe pure air again.

She was pleased with Fahmy, and proud of him. He had sound sense, for one so young; he should go a long way.

The strain on him was not the less great for all his sense. That was what grieved Laila. She heard him stirring about sleeplessly all that night. She listened to him, pacing and mumbling to himself. She wondered: 'Allah knows what is best for you when you yourselves do not,' says the Koran; but what possible good was Fahmy, or any of them, supposed to derive from this ordeal? Towards daybreak, Fahmy's restive movements ceased, and Laila went to sleep.

From that time on, however, the atmosphere even at home, instead of lightening, grew hourly heavier with sullen moodiness. Laila could not make out this new turn: did Fahmy impatiently wish to be free to bring home a mate? Was that it? Or was his waxing surliness symptomatic of a systematic poisoning of his soul by venom-brewing neighbors? Laila was in a dilemma: should she leave? or was it her duty to him to dispel the shadows darkening his life, if that were his trouble? At no time did he give her any opening for explanations or an understanding. His silence kept her silent. Yet, all the while, his smouldering mood grew blacker.

"Why does our brother act as though he hated us?" Fahima one day demanded tremulously.

"Oh, he doesn't! That is just his manner," Laila soothed quickly. But that decided her. The hateful air of their home would soon be affecting the children. Whatever Fahmy was brooding over, Laila's being there was manifestly helping him none; perhaps her going would bring him to himself. She had Mohamed get together everything needful for them to pack up quickly and leave; but in such manner as not to disturb anything until next morning. It was too much to hope that Fahmy might show a brighter spirit even at the eleventh hour; yet Laila wished he might.

If anything, Fahmy was worse that evening on his return, than he had ever been. He glared hatefully whenever he looked toward Laila. The evening meal over, he stalked up abruptly to his feet.

"Did you kill my father? Did you?" he yelled at her. "To regain freedom, you poisoned him! You killed him!" His tirade rose to a hysterical pitch. Laila could only stare, speechless! They all did. They gaped at him in shocked silence until he slunk off, shamefaced but still growling under his breath.

It had been in Laila's mind merely to seek another place in the village, when she had first decided to move; but she now resolved to leave the village altogether. She thought carefully, one by one, of several likely towns: Aswan, Isna, Tahta, Asyut, El Wasta, El Ayat —they were either too near to Nag-Hamadi to serve her purpose, or else their size did not seem to lend plausibility to any excuse she could think of for wishing to travel so far to get there!—Cairo! The Capital flashed for the first time into her mind. It took her breath away. She would have no trouble finding reasons for wanting to go there! And it was far enough away from Nag-Hamadi, surely!

It was decided.

THE momentous next day, from the moment Fahmy left for work, Laila and Mohamed pitched in and packed. The children did what they could, too, jabbering incessantly; and by ten o'clock that morning they were packed and away. They went by train; and though they fairly whizzed through fields, desert and towns, it was a long ride.

Nefissa was no less thrilled to be off to Cairo, than were her sisters, for all her worldly sixteen years. Aziza tried to emulate her older sister's outward calm; but in the end they were all as excited as Fahima, who was a big handful from the start.

The flies were thick, and sticky. They would not have been bothersome if the girls had been able to sit quietly, and let the flies do likewise. But, at first, the children had to watch the flying landscape, and kept jumping around to see all they could. Then Aziza began imagining there was a bug in her clothes; and kept squirming until sly Fahima at last produced one from somewhere and executed it for Aziza to see, whereafter Aziza rested in the comfortable thought that the offender was dead. Then their seats began feeling uncommonly hard; and their muscles commenced aching from confinement for so long. They broke the monotony when they could, by getting down at the big stations along the way. At one such stop, Laila bought them all *fil* for their mid-day meal; they washed this stew pie down with cool drinks of tamarind, served to them directly by the vendor in his clinking brass cups.

It was dark when they pulled into Cairo. Mohamed had a friend in this city. This was fortunate, since none of them knew anything at all about the place. The thought of the size and renown of Cairo, teeming with its tens of thousands, scattered their wits in panic. It seemed, even, that the whole manner of human action and thought differed here from the rest of the world! For, Mohamed had difficulty in merely learning how to go about getting in touch with his friends. By lucky chance a friendly station guard came along. He proved a very geni; and after cross-questioning Mohamed for ten or twenty minutes, got things in motion. They found Mohamed's friend; and he got them a place to spend the night.

Cairo was a terrifying place, at first; it was so huge, with so many temptations and expenses. But within a week, they had all begun to feel safe; and by the end of their first month there, they had learned their way about their immediate neighborhood. The girls quickly picked up some of the ways and expressions of the city. Laila was not sure she approved; it worried her a little. This, and loneliness for old friends, made her think of home many a time. She had intended to cut entirely free from Nag-Hamadi, in coming to Cairo; but in one of her nostalgic fits, she sent off a note to a trusted friend back home, begging for news. She at once confessed this weakness to Nefissa, who traded the avowal with one of her own: all of them had secretly done the very same thing; and Mohamed who had succumbed within twenty four hours of arrival in Cairo, being unschooled, had even got a public scribe to write a letter home for him.

The five of them had probably never sent more than five letters anywhere before, amongst them. Their friends at Nag-Hamadi, not having homesickness to goad them into the literary labor of replying, did not reply.

Then, day of days, there came a letter! Everyone had stopped expecting any; and the surprise was exciting. Laila was alone when she got it. It was from Nag-Hamadi — the postmark on the envelope showed that! News from home at last. Laila, to whom it was addressed, opened it in nervous haste after inspecting the cover. But it turned out to be something else from anything she might have imagined.

Unsigned and in a disguised hand, it was a warning: Fahmy had learned the family's whereabouts. He still raved queerly at times, about his father's "murder."

And he had let it be known in Nag-Hamadi that he was going to Cairo to "avenge" his father's death.

It was all so wild a fancy, that Laila saw how ridiculous this warning letter was. True or false, the contents of such a missive could have been written only by her spiteful ex-neighbor. Would she who was at the seat of Fahmy's tragic foolishness, go so far out of her way as to warn Laila, this way? Laila thought not! But would it not be just like her persecutor to try to disturb Laila's peace of mind even as far away as Cairo? That was more likely!

Three days later, Fahmy arrived.

Laila was stunned a moment by surprise. Then she remembered the anonymous warning. It chilled her blood. All idea was instantly abandoned, of going out now. For Fahmy had arrived just as she and the girls were preparing to leave the house. Laila wanted to give her step-son such heartening welcome as he had never received anywhere before. That would mollify him if he were here on mischief; or reassure him if his visit were a friendly one.

"My dear son! Fahmy!" she smiled, coming forward to meet him. "Come in! You are most welcome here!"

THE girls were overjoyed to see their brother. His smiling gracious bearing eased all recollection of how brooding he had been when last they had seen him.

Led by Laila herself, they escorted Fahmy into the apartment. Their excited chatter was deafening. Mohamed appeared, and gaped; then he, too, joined in the warm welcome to the son of the house. Furniture and personal effects were shifted around in a twinkling; and Fahmy was installed as guest of honor.

All this time, the exiles flung questions at Fahmy. What news of this person or that? What of Zenaib? How was he doing at his shop? How had he spent his time? Fahmy had no chance to get an answer in edgewise until finally Laila's voice prevailed:

"We are all so happy to see you here! Are you moving to the Capital? Or is this only a visit? Tell us all about your plans!"

"Only a visit," said Fahmy. "I had two days off from work, and seized the chance to come and see you."

"You did right! We'll show you the city!" said Aziza joyously.

"I could not know what welcome I might receive here," chided Fahmy gently. "I was as grieved as I was astonished, to come home one evening and find you all silently gone off to settle in Cairo!" At this, Laila bowed her head noncommittally. "But even if you never wrote to let me know it, I am glad to see that you acted that way out of no ill will. Your welcome convinces me of that!"

"My dear son! How could it ever occur to you that there might be ill will in anything we did concerning you!" protested Laila quickly. He was not the ugly stepson she had fled at Nag-Hamadi. She wished to repair their relationship as far as possible. She had been right, too, about that anonymous "warning": its author had patently wished thereby to spoil this chance of reconciliation.

They flung themselves merrily into celebrating the few available hours of Fahmy's visit. He stayed another day to get everything in.

The next day afterward, he still lingered.

"We like to have you!" puzzled Laila. "But it would be most unfair of us to keep you away from your work. That might prejudice your employment. We would not forgive ourselves for that!"

"Have no fear!" Fahmy waved blandly. "I don't think I shall return to Nag-Hamadi, after all. You are right about the advantages of a city of Cairo's size: customers are countless, business is good!"

"Oh, I don't know! Conditions are different here from at home."

"Ah, but I have looked around; and I have found employment here!"

"Oh, I see," Laila nodded. "In that case, you must stay with us—you haven't other plans?"

"No other plans. I'll gladly stay; and thanks!" grinned Fahmy.

There seemed to Laila a furtiveness in Fahmy's slipping off this way, and quietly finding work in Cairo. Coming as a surprise, Fahmy's move was disturbing. The girls, though, were delighted; so Laila made no mention, even to Mohamed, of her uneasiness. As days passed and Fahmy kept her at a distance regarding his plans, Laila's imagination seemed to play her tricks: she fancied more than once that she had caught his eyes upon her with the old-time peculiar glint, and when their eyes unexpectedly met, he would smile like a cat who has just eaten a pet canary.

Thinking it all out carefully after several days of trial, Laila came to another of her spot decisions.

"Mohamed," she bade the next morning as soon as Fahmy had gone. "We are finding a new place to live. Start packing."

"Leaving here!" piped Nefissa. Her sisters chorussed their amazement. But they got busy with their packing. "What will poor Fahmy think when he comes home and finds us gone again?"

"We can't help what he thinks, can we?" countered Laila. "We have our own lives and business to attend to. Your brother takes no pains to conceal that he feels that way, himself, about his own affairs! He has lived with us not as an invited guest so much as like one who has the right to stay here; but has he confided any of his affairs to you, in a brotherly way, or come to me, his mother, with the frankness of a son? No—Anyway, we're moving; and now!"

Mohamed volunteered a diffident endorsement of Laila's judgment, and the three girls accepted their elders' decision without argument.

THEY found a place on the other side of town which suited them perfectly. It was an apartment of four rooms, including a spacious kitchen. Being on the second floor, and at the back, accounted for the reasonable rent: some people would object to such a location, but not Laila. She did not mind the stairs, and she did like being on an outside court, even if only a back court.

The apartment was ideally arranged: a central parlor, two bedrooms and the kitchen. Laila took one of the two rooms off the parlor; and the girls shared the other. Mohamed was apportioned the kitchen, where he would spend most of his working hours and where he would occupy a mattress in a corner at night and siesta-periods. In short order they had their furniture arranged.

Then followed several days of suspense, while they all waited apprehensively to see whether Fahmy would try to find them. Nothing happened, and they relaxed. Each took up life where Fahmy's arrival had interrupted its routine.

After two peaceful weeks, in stalked Fahmy.

He was furious. He minced no words about it. In the full richness of his vocabulary, he upbraided Laila in sixty ways, not once repeating himself, for ditching him shamefully in a strange city. He had come all the way from Nag-Hamadi to be with her and his sisters; and after accepting their pressing invitation to stay with them, he was left meanly in the lurch one fine day!

Beaten in her second evasion, Laila bowed to Fate. She invited Fahmy to come and live with them if he wished. He said that he felt it the only course for him.

"Our space is limited and poorly arranged for guests," Laila told him. "You will have to share the parlor with Mohamed." That seemed pointed enough: assigning him to share an inconvenient room with the domestic. Fahmy accepted, however, without turning a hair; and forthwith moved in.

"Oh, Mohamed," Laila ordered. "When you bring your mattress into the parlor tonight—you understand—arrange a second one for our guest, please. He is stopping with us." Mohamed understood.

The circumstance of Fahmy's current visit was not calculated to enhance the family geniality when they all gathered. Fahmy seemed to be trying to do his best to mend their spirits; his smile was greatly in evidence at all times, he jested often and lightly, and he worked hard to strengthen the blood-ties between himself and his sisters. But something important was lacking: was it sincerity?

Laila mistrusted him in spite of herself. She got Mohamed to bring in a friend who could be trusted to share the responsibility with him, of guarding the household against anything untoward. With the appearance of this reinforcement, Laila felt easier; and the girls sympathetically dropped their nervous reserve.

One evening soon afterward, when supper was over and they were all amusing themselves at their usual recreations, Fahmy rose from the divan where he had been musing to himself.

"I think I'll go out for a while. Don't wait up for me."

Laila sharply watched him go out.

"It's such a beautiful night!" commented Aziza. "Such stars!— Like a rug of diamonds spread on the floor of the heavens by the lavish whim of some *djin!*"

"He must be thinking of staying out late," Laila said half to herself, and added, addressing Mohamed: "I wish you'd keep an eye open until he's safely in bed and asleep"

Fahmy had not got back by nine, nor by ten, nor even by eleven. Laila sent the girls off to their rooms at ten; and was in bed and asleep, herself, by eleven. Mohamed and his friend lay on their mattress-beds in the dark parlor, their talk growing drowsier and drowsier.

THE neighborhood woke dully to a cry in the night; then sharply roused, as shriek after shriek of a woman in mortal terror, died suddenly on the air. A policeman sprinted towards the back courtyard where the cries still echoed. As he reached the spot, a fugitive figure jumped out the second-floor window. The man of Law pounced on him. No need for words: the crouching fellow still held in his hand the tell-tale evidence of his crime and guilt—a hammer, flesh-spattered and slick with gore.

"Drop it!" the policeman barked, drawing his service revolver. The hammer clattered to earth. The policeman promptly snapped handcuffs on his prisoner's wrists, and gave him a sharp push to start him on his way to jail to await trial.

"Huh-ha-ha-hah! — Well, I'm glad of it, anyway!" laughed Fahmy in his captor's face.

THE Law Enforcement Committee of the American Bar Association declares in a recently-issued, interesting and revealing report that:

> A major crime is committed in the United States every twenty seconds.

VENGEANCE OF "THE LAMP POST"

By

James Cunha

"I'LL KILL any pig of a person who says I am not the toughest man in all Brazil!"

Virgolino Ferreira da Silva was roaring drunk. As the patrons in the tavern on the outskirts of Pernambuco scurried for cover, Virgolino puctuated his boast by shooting out the lights in the smoke-filled café, then ended his revolver practice by extinguishing the gas-lamps atop the posts in the road outside.

Thus Virgolino, at the age of 16, came by his nickname of "The Lamp Post," or *Lampeao* in the Portuguese dialect.

It was not long after he made his drunken boast that Virgolino showed his insatiable thirst for blood and began a career of murder and pillage that for years terrified white and native settlers in the steaming jungles.

He lived in the interior of the State of Pernambuco with his father José, four brothers and three sisters. One day, his father told

BRAZIL: *The amazing story of a bandit whose ruthless murders and pillaging so paralyzed the countryside that, after his capture, his severed head and those of his band, were widely displayed to reassure an unbelieving public that his reign of terror was ended.*

him that a neighboring peasant had stolen one of his goats.

"That dog can't do that to us!" the youth exploded. He called his brothers and the five young men strode across the clearing facing José's hut of grass and dried mud. From a cache of a rotting mahogany tree they pulled out a jug of caxaca, an extremely potent firewater brewed from sugar cane.

José paid no attention to his high-spirited brood. By nightfall, the youths had finished the jug and set off through the jungle.

The Lamp Post, who had established his leadership, although he was not the oldest of the five, stopped at another cache. There he distributed four machetes.

"You understand what you're going to do?" *Lampeao* asked his brothers.

The young men nodded.

THREE hours later the quintet straggled back through the jungle, homeward bound. Two of the brothers bore torches to light the way. The fitful light revealed a ghastly procession.

The Lamp Post led the swaying column carrying a pole on which was impaled the grinning head of the goat-stealing neighbor. Others of the da Silva clan followed with the rest of the dismembered body of the guilty peasant. Pedro, the youngest, brought up the rear of the parade leading the goat by a halter in one hand, while in the other he held a second jug of caxaca stolen from the murdered man.

At the slain peasant's home, now but a heap of smouldering embers, desolation reigned. The peasant's wife had the initial "L" branded on both cheeks, and the two daughters, aged 12 and 15, lay on the ground unconscious and brutally beaten.

As the brothers made their way through the jungle, they sang lustily. José heard them coming long before he spied their torches.

Even the grizzled old man, who had swung a mean machete in his time, was taken aback by the appalling ferocity of his sons.

"I don't mind your killing the thief," he remonstrated. "But you didn't have to cart his carcass home in pieces. Throw him in the river, and be quick about it!"

The Lamp Post had tasted blood, and like the beast in the jungle, he could not forget.

The five brothers had left their home for another spree in Pernambuco when a band of desperadoes raided their father's farm in the interior. For some time this gang had been extorting tribute from the settlers. The State Constabulary seemed helpless. In a number of districts, tax collectors could not gather government imposts because the gang had rendered the farmers destitute.

There was reason to suppose that the leader was a friend of the peasant whom the da Silva brood had killed. In any event, old man

José's throat was slit and the three daughters cruelly attacked. When The Lamp Post and his brothers returned from their debauch, they found their father lying in a pool of drying blood and their sisters weeping hysterically in the jungle.

Standing over José's body *Lampeao* swore a terrible oath of vengeance. Even his brothers quaked before his insensate fury.

Their first impulse was to set out in immediate pursuit, and ambush the gang. But The Lamp Post's wiser and craftier counsel prevailed.

"No, you fools, that's idiotic! Do you know what we're going to do? We're going to enlist in the Constabulary!" said *Lampeao.*

Only Pedro, the youngest, had the courage to stand up to his brother.

"How can we do that, Virgolino? The police want us for chopping up that peasant."

"Little cockroach!" snarled The Lamp Post. "They can't hang that on us. There's no evidence. If we offer to enlist, that'll be a sign of our good intentions. Also, we'll get some guns, which is more than we've got now. We'll set off tomorrow at dawn."

Back at Pernambuco, three of the da Silva brood applied at the recruiting office; the other two having declined to join them.

The Lamp Post declared vehemently that while he wanted to avenge his father's murder, he wished to do so "legally."

"Moreover," he declared with convincing patriotism, "this State needs all the able-bodied men it can find to rid itself of these murderers. My two brothers and myself want to do our duty."

The brothers were accepted without further delay. They were assigned to a troop of rookies, undergoing special training in military drill and rifle practice. The Lamp Post showed himself remarkably proficient.

After a month's training he was made an honorary captain, and instructed to patrol a section of the interior. With nine men — including his two brothers — and equipped with ten rifles, as many mounts and enough supplies required for a month's expedition, he set out at the head of his column on March 8, 1918.

"Adios, and good fortune!" his colonel sang out as the little cavalcade started on its way.

That was the last the Pernambuco Constabulary was to see of The Lamp Post for twenty years, save for brief clashes with him and his followers as they escaped through the jungles after sanguinary raids on defenceless farmers.

TWENTY-FOUR hours later, with a safe distance between him and the Constabulary post, The Lamp Post called a council of war. Excepting his brothers, the recruits were ordered to stack their arms and gather around the camp-fire.

"You may as well know now," *Lampeao* declared, grinning hugely, "that you are all relieved of your oaths of allegiance to the crooked government. We're going to rob the countryside, just as the gang did that murdered my father. In six months we'll be rolling in wealth!"

The Lamp Post paused and looked around significantly at the men reclining before the fire.

"Any of you who don't want to join me can leave now!"

There was a murmur of restless comment, while Pedro and Sebastian, standing guard over the stacked rifles, smiled knowingly.

The Lamp Post laughed. "Well, who wants to go? Now's your last chance!"

Two of the recruits arose.

"We'll say nothing to the Constabulary about what you're planning, *Lampeao*," one of them said, but robbing isn't our line. *Adios!*"

The pair, without rifles or horses, started to march off into the jungle. The Lamp Post cooly raised his rifle to his shoulder, aimed deliberately, and drilled both men through the backs of their heads.

There was no more talk of desertion.

Although better equipped than most gangs, due to *Lampeao's* duplicity, the group was weak in numbers. With only eight men he could not hope to rob on any such scale as he had at first dreamed . He realized, too, that, sooner or later, the Constabulary would dispatch a column to arrest him on charges of desertion and theft of government property; and his small troop could not, very well, battle any large force.

Strategy and discretion demanded, therefore, that he join forces with another gang until such time he could launch out for himself.

The Lamp Post learned, through the grape-vine system of the jungle, that a bandit leader named Manuel Porcino, was not averse to enlarging his band. Manuel and Virgolino met up in the Pernambuco hinterland and, both happily unendowed with the slightest scruples, took to each other immediately. They agreed to share profits.

MEANWHILE, the Constabulary did not wait long to dispatch a punitive column after The Lamp Post. An advance party, consisting of a sergeant and two troopers caught up with the combined da Silva-Porcino forces near one of the coastal settlements, which the outlaws had planned to raid.

Unfortunately for the troopers, the bandits saw them first. Shooting from an ambush of tall cactus-plants, The Lamp Post himself killed all three men with his Government rifle and bullets. Instead of retiring into the jungle, the bandit insisted on abiding by the original plan, and led the descent upon the sleeping settlement.

Four men were murdered in their sleep, their heads wrapped in burlap bags, and sent by express mail to the Constabulary commandant at Penambuco. When the colonel opened the package, disclosing the grisly contents, he found a note.

> "This is a reminder," it read, "not to send your toy soldiers after us in the interior. I killed three of your men myself, and we'll kill any others you send up-country. Be warned!"
>
> *"Lampeao"*

The bandit took approximately $5,000 in cash, stock, jewels and other property in the raid on the coastal village. Moreover, in further celebration of his first major operation, The Lamp Post took three young women as hostages, one of them, Maria Bonita, later becoming his favorite mistress and lieutenant. With the other two, he adopted a policy that was to prove characteristic of him in later raids. He branded his initials on their cheeks and arms, and trained them to shoot and ride. They became modern counterparts of the Amazonian female warriors of history, and not the least voracious and cruel of The Lamp Post's growing army.

Porcino was so impressed with his partner's first coup that soon thereafter he decided to retire and to appoint The Lamp Post his successor. Porcino himself had a reputation in the hinterland for ruthlessness, but more than likely his motive for resigning was fear of the even crueller da Silva. The latter had proved himself altogether too capable of putting a bullet in a man whose back was turned.

Now in complete charge of the men, The Lamp Post drilled them after the methods he had learned at the Pernambuco post of constabulary. He foresaw that he would have numerous encounters with Government forces, and was determined not to employ the old, haphazard guerrila tactics, but to fight fire with fire. The women were subjected to the same rigorous training.

The Lamp Post soon developed a novel and bloodless method of scattering the forces of the Constabulary. Once he had decided upon a given town to raid, he would dispatch extortion messages to the merchants of half a dozen communities at a safe distance from his objective. In these missiles, he boldly announced that he would invade these settlements on or around a certain date.

The terrified merchants, whom The Lamp Post was careful to see had learned of his murders and pillages up-country, inevitably summoned the Constabulary. The man-strength of an entire regiment would be scattered in the half-dozen towns, awaiting the arrival of the dreaded bandit.

The Lamp Post, of course, never arrived at any of these communities, or did so rarely. More often than otherwise, when he and his men came to their secret objective at night, with a burst of shooting and blood-curdling yells, there was not a Constabulary officer within miles.

THE men and women robbed at their leisure. Invariably, the leader decapitated at least two or three of his victims. On one such raid, daringly made, not far from Pernambuco, he beheaded six men. Two of the heads he sent as another "souvenir" to the chief officer of the Constabulary.

The other four he kept for dispatch as "warnings" to merchants who delayed sending him their cash tributes by messenger. Others he used to terrify young boys and girls into joining his army. If they refused, The Lamp Post, grinning evilly, would draw one or more heads from a bag, much as a magician draws rabbits from a silk-hat.

The heads were also used by him to freshen the memories of merchants and small bankers who claimed they had no money or valuables, or had "forgotten" where they were kept. These grisly exhibits were invariably effective as spurs to faulty memories.

But one coffee-grower refused to be intimidated in this manner.

"You can't frighten me, you devil!" the plantation owner screamed. "You won't get a penny from me!"

"As you wish, Senhor."

The Lamp Post smiled pityingly, and signalled to his two brothers. They knocked the man to the ground and pinioned him there by stakes through his arms and the fleshy part of his legs.

A day later, the Constabulary found the coffee-grower devoured by red ants. Before leaving his victim, The Lamp Post had one of his women engrave his initials on the man's face. For good measure, the bandits set fire to his crops, and the blaze, spreading to the plantation-house, burned the man's wife and two small children to a crisp.

Maria Bonita was the leader in some of the most atrocious torturing of his victims. She was about 20 when seized by *Lampeao,* a buxom mulatto with an untidy shock of raven hair and a face scarcely less vicious than The Lamp Post's.

"I love a man with guts," she told her companions. "*Lampeao's* a hero. He's not afraid of anyone! . . . Did you see the clever way he chopped that fellow's hand off?"

Most of these tales of The Lamp Post were told by the few men who succeeded in deserting his army. Others were explicit in the bloody evidence that the bandit left behind him.

One of the man's most daring raids, although it did not prove successful, was on a Constabulary outpost near Bahia.

When they learned of his incredibly audacious plan, even The

Lamp Post's brothers protested.

"You're joking!" Pedro exclaimed. "Apart from the risks, what in God's name do you expect to find there?"

"Rifles, you fool! We're running low on ammunition, too."

"Well, why go there of all places! The Constabulary's been hunting for us five years. We'll just be walking into a trap."

The Lamp Post spat in disgust.

"That's where you're wrong, as usual. They'd never think we'd have the nerve to attack them. Anyway, they've not more than a dozen men at that outpost. We'll march after supper."

Maria was delighted over her lover's boldness.

About 150 men encircled the post by midnight, a sort of "pill-box" on the edge of the jungle, guarding one of the approaches to the town. When The Lamp Post gave the order to rush the miniature fortress, machine-gun fire burst out on all sides.

That was a new experience for *Lampeao*. Hitherto, he had usually confronted only farmers armed with old rifles, or totally unarmed women, and but rarely any Constabulary troopers in the forests. He could not cope with machine-guns. He went down, with a bullet in his right eye, and before he could retreat to the safety of the jungle, he had lost six men.

Miraculously, The Lamp Post lived through the experience. He lost his eye but Maria, nursing him day and night, pulled him through. The result of that shattering experience was a redoubled determination to kill more of the Constabulary—and to obtain machine-guns.

He achieved this end by dealing with gun-runners through intermediaries. The cost was high, but paid for by more frequent raids on settlements. The Lamp Post was in the way of becoming the out-law dictator of the State of Pernambuco as well as adjoining districts.

AT this point, about 1928, The Lamp Post was at the height of his power. No predatory denizen of the deepest jungle spelt such terror to natives as the name of *Lampeao*. And ironically, at this time, a well-founded report was circulated that the bandit-leader was dead. Constabulary officers were certain the one-eyed chieftain had been killed in the abortive raid on the "pill-box".

But they and the countryside were soon disillusioned. To the Constabulary commandant came a note:

"If you think me dead, pig, come and get my carcass!" it read.

The crude handwriting and the signature were unmistakable. Inclosed in the letter was a single machine-gun bullet. Evidently that was the Lamp Post's way of suggesting he would welcome the Constabulary warmly!

Now equipped with light machine-guns, carried by stolen mules, *Lampeao* extended his activities. The State of Permanbuco had been fairly well covered by The Lamp Post, and for once he and his followers—Maria Bonita excepted—began to fear the Constabulary of that province. Complaints reached the federal authorities at Rio de Janeiro of new and bloodier raids in the provinces of Bahia, Sergipe, Alagoas, Caera, and Rio Grande del Norte.

To make pursuit more difficult, The Lamp Post now made a habit of forcibly conscripting road laborers, after destroying the projects they were building. Hitherto he had been successful in eluding pursuit largely by reason of the inaccessibility of much of the territory he plundered. But after 1925 the Brazilian government began a vast road-building program.

Over these macadamized highways, armored cars roared in pursuit of the bandit and his army of cutthroats. Several times the crews of these cars almost captured him until he changed his tactics and remained off the roads.

By 1932 he was recognized as Brazil's National Menace No. 1. An elaborately armed and equipped force was dispatched from Rio de Janeiro to bring him back dead or alive, preferably dead. The commander of this hand-picked force was given orders not to return without The Lamp Post, or without positive evidence that he and his lieutenants were dead.

FOR six months, in jungle and on plain, this Federal force followed *Lampeoa's* trail of blood. In June, 1932, the commander believed he had The Lamp Post trapped in the neighborhood of a settlement in Rio del Norte province. The leader had reportedly retreated to a hide-away, an enormous cave, still to be fully explored, the entrance to which was half-way up a cliff that rose almost perpendicularly.

A swiftly-flowing stream ran near the base of the cliff. If the Federal troops could approach the cave unseen by the bandits, they might smoke them out with tear gas and massacre them individually as they fled from the entrance.

The plans of the federal troopers were made with the minutest attention to detail. Shortly before midnight, traveling afoot, they crossed the stream a mile above the site of the cavern, and made their way downstream on the opposite bank.

The Federals took an hour to cover the mile to a point below the cave. Every precaution was taken against making any sound. The task was both hazardous and difficult, since the force of fifty men was equipped not only with rifles, but also with ten machine-guns and a quantity of tear-gas bombs. A false move might cause The Lamp Post to rake the narrow path, leading up to the cave-entrance, with a murderous fire.

Spies in neighboring settlements had told the Federal officers that armed men had been seen climbing to the hide-out. Their descriptions were so detailed that the government officers had no doubt that they were approaching one of the bandits' hiding-places.

Advancing inches at a time, the men were deployed about the yawning mouth of the cave. Now working rapidly, the ten machine-guns were mounted to command the entrance with a sweeping fire.

The commander rose from his crouch. He could not control his excitement.

"Now, men, get the dogs!"

Simultaneously, a dozen tear-gas bombs were hurled at the entrance, and a portable searchlight trained on the spot. Suddenly, government men heard roars and screams within, as of men and women in agony. Through a megaphone the commander shouted:

"Come out, you devils! One by one, without your guns!"

But no human answered the command. As additional persuasion, the entrance was subjected to a few bursts from the machine-guns. At this, a huge panther, her infuriated mate and three cubs dashed out to the ledge, blinded by the searchlight and spitting and snarling from the gas.

Several aditional bursts from the guns were fired before the troopers were ordered to advance.

Inside the damp an.l long cave the soldiers found the partially devoured bodies of four men!

There was evidences that The Lamp Post and his men had lately visited the cave. Officials later learned he used the place occasionally as a sort of "jungle mortuary" for those of his victims who proved obdurate. After shooting them, he had the bodies dumped in the cave, which was often visted at night by beasts of the jungle.

That method was more convenient than burying those he slew. Moreover, it was safer than leaving the bodies in the jungle where vultures gathering above would inform settlers and constabulary that The Lamp Post was probably in the neighborhood.

BUT Federal and constabulary forces were closing in on *Lampeoa.* Many settlers and farmers had fled from the interior, so that for food and other supplies the bandit was forced to approach the more populated coastal communities. To hasten his capture the Rio de Janeiro authorities posted a reward of $5,000.

Early this year, the constabulary of the State of Alagoas, one of several which The Lamp Post had overrun, determined to win the reward. With a posse of infuriated farmers, they trapped him near the village of Villanova, about 250 miles north of San Salvador in the State of Bahia, the constabulary of which joined forces with that of Alagoas.

In a three-hour guerilla battle, The Lamp Post, eleven of his henchmen, and Maria Bonita were killed. She was operating a machine-gun when one of the militia bullets lodged in her throat. One Federal trooper was killed.

But Brazilians would not believe the first reports that One-Eyed Lamp Post was dead — he had been reported slain before. So, following the example of the gang, the constabulary enthusiastically beheaded the twelve men and one woman they had killed!

They brought the heads of the thirteen to headquarters of the Alagaos Constabulary, and arrayed them symetrically on four shelves, with some of their plunder and arrms as added *décora.*

Peasants were freely permitted to view the gruesome exhibit, and many of them spat on the head of The Lamp Post, who occupied the place of honor, on the first bloodstained shelf, immediately below that of his mistress. Many of the witnesses had lost sons and daughters, husbands and wives, because of the leader's ruthless warfare.

After the thirteen grisly heads rested in "state" for several days, the central government ordered photographs taken of the appalling exhibit. These were distributed to newspapers throughout Brazil —reassuring evidence to tens of thousands of readers that the terrorist was dead.

But the spectacular execution of The Lamp Post and his companions was not to end the fearful banditry to which Brazil had been exposed for a score of years. The excitement had scarcely abated, and farmers peacefully recovered their settlements in the hinterland, when the bandit scourge again made itself felt.

On the night of August 3, 1938, six human heads were tossed on the steps of the headquarters of the Alagoas Constabulary. Attached to the bag containing the heads was a scrawled note signed by one Corisco, the most bloodthirsty of The Lamp Post's lieutenants. He, with a score of others, had escaped the Federals' bullets at the ambuscade near Villanova.

One of the heads was identified as that of the grandfather of Constabulary Lieutenant Bezerra, who had been chiefly instrumental in the capture of *Lampeoa.* The note stated that Corisco intended to terrorize the country beyond any of The Lamp Post's bloodiest designs, to avenge his death.

THE Brazilian Federal and State police are under no illusions as to the time it may take to capture Corisco and his gang. It took them 20 years to catch The Lamp Post, and before they succeeded the bandit had killed over one hundred men, women and children, and stolen at least $100,000 in cash and property.

THE COBRA WOMAN

By

M. N. Lamarr

THE CALM of the police sub-prefecture of the Kuppelwiesergrasse quarters of Vienna was broken by the shrill, persistent ring of the phone early in the morning of October 31, 1936.

"Yes?" asked the desk sergeant, suppressing a yawn.

"This is Frau Martha Marek of No. — Kuppelwiesergrasse," a breathless voice informed him. "My home has been robbed! Send someone quick!"

The chief of police was informed and he assigned Inspector Rudolf Peternell to investigate the case. Peternell had a particularly naive facial expression and a stupid manner, yet this youngest plainclothesman on the Vienna police force was considered unusually intelligent; the loutish manner he employed being solely a disguise to disarm suspicion.

The Inspector hurried to the home of Frau Marek and found her in a semi-hysterical state; she appeared to be genuinely upset. Indeed, he could hardly help but sympathize with her. She seemed to be blind in one eye, walked with a decided limp and her left arm dangled lifelessly at her side, apparently paralyzed.

"This is terrible, young man!" she sobbed, tears streaming down her handsome face. "Last night I sent my maid to the cinema, and I retired early. When the maid returned from the theater, she

AUSTRIA: *The case of "the devil in petticoats" whose long career of crime went unnoticed by the Viennese police, until a trivial charge of fraud brought to light a series of diabolical murders.*

went straight to her room and says she did not notice anything out of the ordinary."

"Well, what happened then?" prodded the Inspector.

"When I came downstairs this morning," Frau Marek continued, dabbing her eyes, "and entered my drawing room, all my tapestries had been ripped from the wall and all my beautiful paintings were gone. Most of my jewelry also has been stolen. Come, I'll show you."

"Just a minute, Madame—didn't you hear any noise during the night?" inquired the young man.

"No, indeed! Ever since I had a paralytic stroke a while ago I have slept very heavily. Come—" she added, leading the way into the other room.

The detective examined the drawing room and the rest of the apartment. He did not ask the woman to explain why the robbers had made off with such cumbersome articles as tapestries and paintings, while they had not elected to steal the large quantity of expensive silverware, which was plainly in sight.

As though the question was a perfunctory one, he asked, "Are you insured?"

"Certainly. I took out a policy against fire and theft for 12,000 schillings with the agent, Jeno Neumann. But it will not cover my losses. They will amount to fully 15,000 schillings."

It seemed to the detective that Frau Marek was too glib about her insurance. Moreover, he recalled reading in society columns that the woman had recently been seen in several of Vienna's gayest cabarets, which did not square with her complaint of a paralytic stroke.

AS IN many American cities, detectives in Vienna work in pairs. Peternell, aided by Detective Josef Gunacker, discovered from the building-agent that a truck had removed a number of large bundles from the Marek apartment a few nights before. On checking the date, they found the truck had called on the night Frau Marek complained she had been robbed.

"And there was nothing wrong with her physically that night," the superintendent concluded. "No paralyzed arm, and she could see as well as I."

To make certain of this, the authorities sent a policewoman to the Marek home, to pose as a substitute for the regular charwoman, who had been induced to feign a serious illness. The woman detective soon reported that Frau Marek was in superb health and rare high spirits; no paralyzed arm, no limp.

The police now had some fruitful bits of evidence of deliberate fraud in connection with her insured art objects. Their clinching discovery was the address of a warehouse where the woman had hidden the tapestries and paintings which she had reported stolen.

Martha Marek had blundered —the police had an open-and-shut case against her.

Unfortunately for Frau Marek, she had a notorious and unsavory reputation in connection with all sorts of queer doings — she had even been accused of murdering her first husband, and her second; of poisoning her child and other people as well. And so it was natural that Inspectors Peternell and Gunacker were not satisfied to let the woman stand trial for the less serious charge of fraud.

For safe-keeping, they jailed her on the fraud charge, while, with all the Viennese astuteness for even the most trivial details, they began to delve deeply into her past.

Questioning hundreds of persons and prying into court files, they pieced together the lurid past of a veritable she-devil beyond the wildest imagination. The story shocked not only Vienna, but all of Europe.

CONCEIVABLY, Martha began life inauspiciously. Though she was born illegitimately, it did not affect her future social standing; a love-child in Europe does not suffer the stigma customary on this side of the Atlantic. The date of her birth was 1898, and its place was Sopron, Hungary.

Martha, as an infant, did not long remain with her mother. Her father had disappeared, and the child was cared for by a chef and his wife. They were a kindly couple, but, harrassed by their own brood of children, by high taxes and the multitudinous social injustices of the then tottering Empire of the Hapsburgs, Martha did not have the care and training of some of her playmates.

Yet she was not a fractious youngster, and she was willing and eager to help her adopted mother in the kitchen. The adoption was not legalized, so that she saw her own mother as often as she wished.

Soon after Martha began school her mother married and, for a woman of her station, seemed to have made a promising match. The husband was one Rudolf Loewenstein, then the station-master at Baden, not far from Vienna. A petty official of that category enjoyed a certain amount of prestige and security, thus he granted the request of his bride to have the little girl live with them.

The hard-pressed chef and his *hausfrau* were willing to relinquish the child, although they had grown fond of the flaxen-haired, pretty-mannered little girl. They gave her up only in the belief that the Loewenstein menage could do more for her than they.

Unfortunately for Martha, the railroad functionary was more ambitious than most of his colleagues. One night he told his wife he was going to the corner *weinstuben* for a glass of Pilsner . . . a month later his spouse received a card from him, mailed from the United

States, where, he wrote, he had gone to make his fortune. He would send for her and Martha, then 7, as soon as he could raise their steerage fare in this land where opportunity and money seemed everywhere.

That was the last heard of the foster-father. Exit from the scene Station-Master Loewenstein.

WITH THE disappearance of her husband, Frau Loewenstein was left virtually without a schilling. She succeeded in placing the child with the Sisters of the Infant Jesus Convent in Vienna. There Martha lived five innocent years, and the growing girl was happy and well cared-for. She was a normally intelligent pupil, popular with both the nuns and her fellow-students.

When she left the convent, at the age of 12, she was very pretty, with the luxuriant fair hair and blue eyes of the typical Viennese. Her figure, even then, was somewhat mature for her age, giving more than a hint of its voluptuous outline of a few years later.

But the chief physical quality about her was an arresting light in the blue eyes. They tell the tale that she could hold the gaze of the convent cat for as long as she pleased. But doubtless, the sisters felt, that was some childish idiosyncrasy that could be rectified with a pair of glasses.

But Martha, it soon became clear, had no thought of wearing anything so disfiguring to her pretty face as spectacles. She was no sooner free of the convent—her skirts not yet below her knees and the radiant hair still resting on her childish shoulders—when she had her first amorous encounter.

Frau Loewenstein, to make ends meet, had placed Martha in a dressmaking shop as an errand girl. Here the impressionable child was confronted with the silken luxuries that money could buy. The contrast between her drab, black dress and thick cotton stockings, and the chic creations of Viennese couturiers hanging in the racks, was not lost on her. Normally enough she wondered: How can these be mine?

She had seen women come into the shop escorted by men who did not act towards them in the manner that husbands usually treated their wives. And Martha decided, precociously, upon an experiment.

The head *vendeuse* of the establishment sent her to deliver a frock to a well-to-do quarter of Vienna. On the street-car she noticed a middle-aged man, prosperously dressed, who was frankly staring at her knees. But instead of feeling any embarrassment or resentment, Martha enjoyed the man's scrutiny. He gave the child a sense of power. When he descended from the street-car at her stop, she accepted his offer of a piece of pastry.

If it sounds ridiculous to say that at the age of 13, a jelly roll started Martha on her sanguinary career, consider the succession of events.

At the café where they stopped, the man introduced himself. He was Moritz Fritsch, owner of one of the most profitable department stores in the Austro-Hungarian capital. Well preserved for his age —he was 62—he was undeniably impressive. Wealth exuded from the glitter of a diamond stick-pin, an expensive ring and a heavy gold watch-chain that glowed across his waistcoast.

Herr Direktor Fritsch disarmed any suspicions that the girl may have had by asking to meet her mother. The result of that interview was Martha's departure from Frau Loewenstein's home to live in the imposing Fritsch mansion at Moedling, as the magnate's ward, with the provision that Herr Fritsch would give the girl a good education.

The education he accorded her, however, was not restricted to the traditional Three R's. The Herr Direktor, divorced since 1900, fell for Martha with all the ardor of a second young-manhood. Indeed, so infatuated was he that he consented to bring into his home the half-sister of his "ward," Paula, whom he also sent to school.

The only fly in the domestic ointment was that Fritsch's adult son and daughter, with considerable justification, smelled a scandal. For scarcely a week after Martha had entered the home, she and her protector were living together as man and wife, despite the difference of almost fifty years in their ages.

The son and daughter demanded her immediate expulsion. When the old man refused, the grown children left their home — and Herr Fritsch was alone with his 13-year-old mistress.

NOW, MARTHA'S insensate career might have been partly explained if the girl had suffered the wartime privations that hundreds of thousands of Austrians were to experience in 1914-18. But she was not undernourished during those four, long, terrible years. She did not want for clothes. The enamoured Herr Direktor, naturally, had less money during the war, yet, at the time of the collapse of the Central Powers, Martha was in radiant beauty and health.

At the age of 21, the gold of her hair had somewhat deepened; she wore it in two shining braids around her small, delicately modelled head. The eerie expression in the eyes, deeply luminous and intent, was slightly more pronounced than in the days, long ago, when she used to transfix the convent cat. The only suggestion of latent cruelty in the face—and it was remote—was the thin, tight lips that belied her passionate nature.

The aging Fritsch, in whom the former *midinette* had long since lost interest, was proud to squire her around the festive cafés that comprised the night-life of the Paris of Central Europe. And if he suspected she was untrue to him, he was philosopher enough to hold his peace.

Then, conveniently, Fritsch died. The end came in 1923 when the store-owner was 74 and Martha a restless and alluring 25. In his last years the old man had suffered from insomnia.

It was then that Martha first became a subject of professional interest to the police. They had received several anonymous letters charging the "ward" with excessive zeal in administering sleeping powders to her guardian.

Officials went to the family survivors and, exhibiting the letters, asked for permission to exhume the body. But the family—even the resentful two children—refused for two reasons: one was religious, the other was their anxienty that exhumation of the body might disclose a crime that would scandalize the city and offend the conventional clientele of the Fritsch store.

This was Martha's first circumvention of the authorities. As Herr Fritsch's common-law wife she inherited a substantial share of his estate. For a girl born illegitimately, with only a smattering of formal education and no background of breeding, she had done well for herself. She was in possession of a mansion and its furnishings, she had enough money to live comfortably, and she had beauty. Life should have appeared idyllic to her.

Mourning contrasted smartly with her fair coloring, but Martha had no intention of grieving excessively for Herr Direktor Fritsch. Three months was more than sufficient. At the end of that period she married Emil Marek.

Marek was 20, the son of bourgeois Viennese parents who were sending him to the Vienna Technical College for a degree in engineering.

He was a brilliant student, and Martha had had the perception to recognize in him an inventive genius. But she regarded his continued schooling as a waste of time, and persuaded her young husband to leave his classrooms. The youth was somewhat erratic, but he nearly put over an engineering coup that would have made him wealthy for life.

This was a project for the electrification of Burgenland, an eastern province that had been devastated by the ravages of war. The Austrian Government was receptive to the idea, novel in many of its conceptions, but officials asked the young inventor to share the risk. It would underwrite ten billion schillings, then about $700,000, if the designer of the project could raise a similar amount.

Precisely at this time, in 1925, Martha Marek displayed an interest in the insurance business that was to remain with her—significantly—for a number of years.

On May 25th of that year the Mareks negotiated an insurance policy for the husband amounting to $400,000, an enormous sum by European standards. The Anglo-Danubian Lloyd Company of Vienna was to pay him that amount in the event of permanent disability; in the event of death, his widow was to receive $100,000.

Incredibly, on May 26th, twenty-four hours after the policy was signed and Marek had paid his first instalment of $870 on the yearly premium, the engineer was permanently disabled. Reasonably, the insurance company felt there was something odoriferous about the entire business, and it began an inquiry into the circumstances of the accident.

The facts, as given by the Mareks to the police, were these:

Marek was chopping wood in the yard of the Moedling mansion with a freshly sharpened hatchet. The tool slipped from his hand, moist with perspiration, and entered his left leg just below the knee. His screams of pain brought Martha and her sister, Paula, racing to the scene. They hurriedly summoned a neighborhood doctor and he, seeing that the foreleg hung to the knee only by a mangled muscle, completed the amputation.

The story might have been plausible, under ordinary circumstances, since the victim, his wife and sister-in-law were all letter-perfect in their accounts of the accident. But it was all too slick, and the newspapers made something of a *cause célèbre* of the "$400,000 leg". Why had the Mareks been in such a hurry to obtain the policy? Why had they taken out so large a sum? And why, finally and most inexplicably of all, had the accident occurred the day after the first premium had been paid?

AT THIS juncture, Martha showed herself considerably less than clever. While the insurance company's inquiry was still under way, she exercised her strong powers of persuasion on one Karl Mraz, a callow youth who had formerly been an orderly in the hospital to which Marek had been taken.

Mraz consented to testify at the forthcoming trial—the insurance company having complained of fraud—that he had overheard the hospital doctors say that they had made Marek's leg appear as though it had been hacked at several places. He further agreed to swear that the doctors had predicted among themselves that they would be generously compensated by Anglo-Danubian Lloyd's.

The aim of this perjured testimony, of course, was to invalidate the charges of fraud. If Mraz told his story convincingly, the Mareks would collect.

Vienna is noted for its efficient

organization of police spies, both men and women. They frequent the cafés, get into homes as domestics, work in hair-dressing establishments, clubs, railroad stations and even operate taxi-cabs. One of this ubiquitous fraternity heard of the proposed testimony, with the result that the Mareks and Mraz were promptly arrested for conspiring to defraud the company.

Fortunately, for the Mareks, the case did not come to trial for many months. In that time public opinion reversed itself. No one believed that a sane man would deliberately chop off his own leg, and it was as grotesque to suppose that a young wife would do it.

One of the dramatic climaxes of the trial was the introduction of "Exhibit 12-A"—Marek's left leg, which the State had preserved in alcohol.

The gruesome evidence caused some score of women in the packed courtroom to keel over as so many nine-pins. Even the hardened judges and court attaches averted their gaze. Martha was the least moved of anyone.

Medical experts disagreed whether it would have been possible for Marek to chop off his leg. On April 7th, 1927, a shout arose in the tense courtroom as the judges found the couple not guilty of conspiracy to defraud. But they were judged guilty of an attempt to corrupt Mraz, and were sentenced to serve four months each in jail. However, since they had spent more than that period in cnofinement awaiting trial, they were released immediately.

The hapless Mraz, a pawn in Martha's game, was sentenced to six weeks for having listened to the Marek's proposals. The insurance company did not get off so lightly, and settled for 180,000 gold schillings, roughly $50,000. The Mareks paid more than half of that sum to their lawyer, the famous Hermann Krazna, and after paying other expenses had a balance of about 30,000 schillings.

The pickings had not been so profitable, but Martha had an eye for business. An idea came to her when, after the verdict had been announced, police had to clear the way to her carriage through cheering crowds shouting congratulations. Martha profitably exploited public and newspaper clamor by appearances at a number of cabarets and, for a limited engagement, even graduated into the ranks of a Johann Strauss operetta.

Meanwhile, Emil Marek had bought a small taxi fleet, but, crippled and unable to supervise the chauffeurs who cheated him, the venture failed. Martha persuaded him that they might do better in North Africa, and for a period of several months he worked for a radio corporation in Algiers. But there bad luck pursued him and, in 1930, they returned to Vienna to open a vegetable market. Eventually, this venture also failed.

By this time, it was clear to their few intimates, that Martha had grown weary of Emil. With but one leg he was not the most romantic object, and far more a hindrance than a help in the economic struggle for a living in post-war, poverty-stricken Austria. Further, to complicate her life, a son had been born in 1930, whom she named Alphons, and three years later there had followed a daughter, Ingeborg.

To save expenses, Emil ate his meals with his parents, after the birth of the second child. This was agreeable to Martha and she appeared glad to be rid of her husband for a few hours each day. But in July she had a change of heart, it seemed, and peremptorily demanded his return to the family hearth. It was not right, she argued, that a husband and wife be separated at the time of breaking bread.

Here we must return briefly to the time of Martha's incarceration while awaiting trial on the fraud charges. In Jail she had met the notorious Leopoldine Lichtenstein, who was charged with murdering her husband through the agency of a rodent poison containing thallium.

The prison matron noted that the two women frequently had their heads together and kept apart from the garden variety of women prisoners — prostitutes, shoplifters and lesser fry.

IN JULY, then, Emil returned to spend all his time with his wife and two children. Overnight he became strangely and seriously ill. In a few days he lost thirty pounds, his hair fell out and, still more mysterious, he went totally blind. Martha was convincingly anxious over her husband's condition when doctors called and ordered him taken to a hospital.

There, on July 31st, the one-legged inventor died. On the death certificate the cause was written as tuberculosis. The rapid loss of weight made that diagnosis reasonable and he had been constitutionally weakened, moreover, by the loss of his leg.

No one, at the time, suspected Martha, despite the fact that Herr Fritsch had died rather mystifyingly and despite some of the malodorous testimony at her trial for fraud. But the fact remained that, when Herr Fritsch became unnecessary to her happiness, he had died, and similarly that when Herr Marek grew useless to her, he also went to his reward.

Evidently, Martha's success at eluding and outwitting the police emboldened her. She envisaged a return of her carefree existence after Fritsch's death when she had no concern other than devising means of amusing herself. But, there was still an obstacle in the way. Two, in fact.

The children, of course!

Ingeborg was but seven months old when she suddenly died. Again as in the case of Fritsch and Emil Marek, the precise cause of death eluded the doctors.

A few days later the 3 year old son, Alfons, was also taken ill and for hours unable to cease vom- his life was saved. A pathetic fact, afterward disclosed, was learned iting. By extraordinary measures through the small boy, who said: "I didn't think I was going to live very long. Mother told me I would go to heaven soon."

It is a cause for some astonishment that neither the police nor the hospital authorities grew suspicious over the three deaths that had occurred in the woman's immediate family, to which should be added the nearly fatal illness of the small boy. Their inability to put two-and-two together was to cost at least two more lives.

Obviously, Martha now regarded herself as invulnerable. But for the next two years she restrained her murderous instincts. Then, in 1934, she launched a campaign to ingratiate herself into the affections of her great-aunt by marriage, Frau Suzanne Loewenstein, then 67, and widow of an Austrian Army surgeon.

The elderly woman was not lovingly disposed either to the Rudolf Loewenstein, Martha's step-father who had run off to America, nor to Martha Loewenstein-Fritsch-Marek.

Yet, so persuasive was the younger woman, that Aunt Suzanne, lonely in her widowhood, became genuinely fond of Martha within a few weeks and made the grandniece her sole heir—thus digging her own grave by her kindness.

A fortnight after Aunt Suzanne's will had been changed, the old woman became gravely ill. There was a very obvious parallel between her symptoms and those of Emil Marek. The widow, until that time unusually robust for one of her age, lost her hair overnight, lost her eyesight, lost the use of her legs.

On July 11th, 1934, Aunt Suzanne was dead.

Again the myopic police failed to see anything unusual in the predilection to death of persons closely associated with Martha Marek.

As the sole heir of Aunt Suzanne's estate, Martha acquired another stake. She gave up her Moedling home and leased a pretentious apartment on the Kuppelwiesergrasse. Here she entertained on a lavish scale and, when her funds were exhausted, took as lover and star-boarder a 49 year old insurance agent named Jeno Neumann.

The liaison of this ogress and Neumann began in 1935, when Martha was 37 and still a woman of decided — and fatal — charms. If she had been able to twist Fritsch, Marek and Aunt Suzanne around her little finger, she exercised an even greater spell over the insurance agent. He was her complete slave, eager to do whatever she asked. There is enough evidence to suggest that she had the power to hypnotize him at will.

It was all of two years since Aunt Suzanne had died and Frau Marek began to feel that she had been inactive overlong. Her next step was to advertise a room suitable for "a middle-aged lady". Frau Felicitas Kittenberger, a seamstress of 53, swallowed the bait and took the room.

The tired little seamstress was visibly impressed by Martha's *grande-dame* manners, her sophistication and knowledge of fashionable Vienna. Martha told her all the gossip of the upper social stratus, real and fancied.

Frau Kittenberger was flattered. Frau Marek, she thought, was an accomplished and suave woman of the world; whatever she said must be gospel.

After a few weeks, Martha went to work on her lodger. She urged her to take out an insurance policy. Neumann extended a fountain pen and a 5,000 schilling life policy before she had time to say no. Martha consented to pay the first premium as a "favor" to her lodger. It was the kiss of death. The unworldly seamstress did not realize that the policy was made out to bearer, and that the bearer was her landlady, Martha Marek.

In a few days the inevitable occurred. Frau Kittenberger fell ill. The usual symptoms appeared —loss of eyesight, paralysis of the legs, loss of hair. On June 1st she was rushed to the hospital, and the day following she breathed her last. Four days later Frau Marek blandly applied for the insurance —and received it.

AGAIN, she told herself, she had fooled the simple-minded police, the coroner and the hospital staff.

But the dead woman's son, Herbert Kittenberger, was far from satisfied. He entered the Kuppelwiesergrasse house and boldly called Frau Marek a murderess and a thief. She summoned the police and had the youth arrested for criminal libel. After listening to his story, the authorities released him.

The police and the prosecutor's office began to wonder if there could be something to the boy's grave charges. Could it be possible that some tremendous blunder had been committed? They made a single dossier of the woman's record. Seen as a whole, the case was black against her; yet there was nothing which could be called reasonable grounds for her arrest on suspicion of murder.

Obviously, they recognized, she was a forceful and ingenious creature, quite capable of vigorously pushing a suit for false arrest. But she would bear watching. Meanwhile, Martha was still enjoying a sense of security and began to look around for new sources of income when the profits of the Kittenberger murder were dissipated.

So it was, then, that the police soon heard from her again in the matter of the house theft, and this time they were on the alert. When Inspectors Peternell and Gunacker, who, it will be recalled, had begun a thorough investigation of Frau Marek's past, had pieced together the terrible trail of this arch murderess, they obtained permission to exhume the bodies of Emil Marek, the infant Ingeborg, Aunt Suzanne Loewenstein and Frau Kittenberger. In every instance they found in the bodies a quantity of thallium which, in paste form, is sold as a rat poison in Vienna.

Finally, a charge of murder was brought against Martha, and the trial, repeatedly postponed, began in June, 1937. On the witness stand she had a trick of staring at the prosecutor which finally so nettled him that the official, at one point of the proceedings, cried out:

"Frau Marek, don't you try to hypnotize me!"

So obstreperous was she on the stand that on several occasions she was found guilty of contempt of court and sent to solitary confinement for twelve hours, to cool off.

When expert witnesses testified, in her defense, that she was unbalanced mentally and that she experienced sexual excitement in watching her victims die of slow poisoning, she could not contain herself and fell into paroxysms of fury. State psychiatrists claimed she was not insane, and that she was—and is—in full possession of a conscience, that she knows right from wrong.

Urged to confess, in order to get a lighter sentence, she screamed at the judges: "You wouldn't believe me anyhow!" The testimony of two druggists that she had repeatedly purchased tubes of rat poison—sufficient to poison half of Vienna—she branded as a tissue of lies. Evidence introduced to prove that Frau Kittenberger had become ill after eating at her home were lightly dismissed by Martha with the flippant remark: "Other people also become sick after meals!"

During her trial, Nazi newspapers sought to make her crimes "credible" by claiming that her antecedents were Jewish, thus removing any stigma on "Nordicks." Her defense lawyers, however, conclusively disproved the charge that she is non-Aryan.

Summarizing the State's case against her, the Prosecutor declared that the "unjust acquittal in the leg amputation trial a decade ago was the death warrant for the four poison victims. She is a cobra in whom the devil lives!"

(*Continued on page* 128)

THE LAST OF "THE INVINCIBLES"

A CRIME CLASSIC

By

Paul Allenby

TWO men walked slowly along the main road that led through Phoenix Park in Dublin. Their conversation was in low tones and the shorter of the two, heavy set of body and square of face seemed to be doing most of the talking. The other man, rather thin-faced and bearded, carried himself with a more patrician air, as though the poise of generations of blue blood had put steel into his straight backbone. He would nod now and then and glance around at the people enjoying the late evening coolness of Phoenix Park.

The shorter man was Thomas Henry Burke, Under Secretary, a British official hated and feared by the bulk of the Irish people. The taller, bearded man was Lord Frederick Cavendish, the newly appointed Chief Secretary and representative of Her Majesty's Gov-

IRELAND: *This historic case of assassination, while little known in America, is familiar to all Irishmen who can recall the struggles of their country for economic and political freedom from British rule. Space does not permit a detailed account of events which lead up to the crimes told in these pages. Suffice it to say, that, during the many years of resistance by the Irish people, much blood was shed on both sides. The case of "The Invincibles", while only one classic example, is of great importance as an indication of the strong feelings during those turbulent days.*

ernment to the Emerald Isle.

Only this morning of May 6, 1882, Lord Cavendish had arrived at Kingstown. Prime Minister Gladstone had removed former Chief Secretary W. E. Forster a few days before. It had been hailed as a smart move that presaged happier relations between Queen Victoria's Government and recalcitrant Ireland.

Frederick Cavendish had no illusions about the difficult task that confronted him. He knew that he could accomplish little in the short space of normal life, that would ease the 600 years of strife between England and the Emerald Isle.

Yet he smiled as he walked through Phoenix Park with his assistant. His heart had thrilled at the ovation the Irish had given him as he had driven from Kingstown to Dublin Castle with his official party. Banners and bunting and flags had decked the triumphal arches through which he had passed. Perhaps he could undo some of the iniquity of Buckshot Forster, as the Irish had contemptuously termed his predecessor.

And it was on this angle of the Irish problem that his conversation with Burke centered.

"WE must reach some peaceable working agreement, Burke," Cavendish said, "with the political groups in Ireland."

Burke smiled crookedly. "I am afraid, your Excellency, that the only agreement that can be reached with an Irishman, especially the men who form the Land League and the Fenians, will have to be first suggested with a gun. These men will go to any end to settle the question—but in their own way. They will not listen to reason, sir."

Lord Cavendish frowned. "Perhaps, Mr. Burke too many guns, too much forcible argument has been used. Perhaps we have been unfair, did you ever think of that? These people are not savages. They are of a different temperament than we in England, but tractible if properly handled. I tell you, Burke, there will be no violence while I am here. At least, it will not be violence that can be considered as emanating from the Government. I am here to make a peace and I intend doing it."

Cavendish was emphatic in his tone. It was evident that he meant, honestly, to try to do something about the Irish situation. Burke's smile faded and for a few minutes the two men walked silently through Phoenix Park.

On one side a cricket match was in progress. A few scattered spectators cheered occasionally. On the other side of the road a polo match was entering its final stages, watched by another handful of fans. Light was beginning to fade as the sun sank fast toward the horizon.

The two men were passing the Viceregal Lodge and were nearing the intersection where they were to turn. Low shrubbery and closer spaced trees lined their side of the road but they could still hear the voices of promenading citizens on the other side of the shrubs. They neared a break in the natural fence where, no doubt, youngsters had often passed chasing a rolling ball, disdaining the more circuitous trip around the shrubbery.

It was getting darker. As they neared the opening in the shrubbery, Lord Cavendish turned slightly toward it, some inner sense of warning making him stop. He saw the men even before Burke, who had gone on a step or two, realized that his superior was not beside him.

How many men there were Lord Cavendish, nor Burke, never lived to remember. Steel flashed in the dimming rays of the sun. Knives slashed down against the two Government officials and the only words that were uttered came in the strident tones of one man in the group: "Ah, you villian!"

They were fateful words, eventually to lead authorities to the men responsible for the double assassination. Burke fell to the ground with several knife wounds in his chunky body. One blade penetrated through his back and cut into his heart, protruding through to the other side. Two other slashes hacked his chest and a fourth and fifth jab hacked his throat. He died almost instantly, blood staining in profusion the grass beneath his body.

Lord Cavendish struggled as best as he could, but the odds were too great. One knife went into the upper part of his shoulder, severing the subclavian artery and he fell to the greensward, a gory mess.

When help finally arrived, Burke was dead. Lord Cavendish died a few minutes later at Stevens Hospital.

IRELAND was a seething volcano of outraged passions in that year of 1882. Street brawls, between constabulary and citizens and between partisans themselves were commonplace. The sensible and cautious Irishman adopted an attitude of minding his own business. The people in the Park, on the recreation grounds watching the cricket and polo games, saw the attack and the attendant scuffle, but, as later investigation showed, they thought it no more than an ordinary street brawl in which they had neither the interest nor the inclination to interfere.

Before anyone sensed what actually had happened, and it was all a matter of a very few minutes, the assassins had fled, some leaving in a private carriage and others dashing off in a waiting hansom cab.

This much the police, under

Chief Superintendent John Mallon, ascertained. Descriptions of the attackers were sketchy and of no use to the authorities. Those who might have seen any one of the attackers were silent at the beginning of the investigation. There was no such thing, then, as a friendly witness.

The English Government, shocked by the murders, promptly reverted to its previous policy. Ireland became bedlam. Raids followed upon raids. Thousands of men and women were arrested and later released for lack of evidence.

A new Crimes Bill was passed to add to the irritation of years of injustice and persecution. A reward of $50,000 was offered and a free pardon for information. Autocratic powers were conferred upon judges, trial by jury being held in abeyance. The Government suppressed all public meetings and gagged the press.

The crime shocked the entire world, but in all justice it was even a greater shock to Irish leaders. Parnell, Davitt and Dillon immediately issued a manifesto to the Irish people, condemning the deed and expressing the hope that the miscreants would soon be apprehended. They termed the crime a stain on the hospitality of the Irish people.

But these were empty words and empty actions. The Irish people viewed such crimes with a different eye. The assassins were secretly looked upon as patriots.

We must now go back to November, 1881, for the beginning of the organization that was to figure so infamously in the murders at Phoenix Park and to the man who was to become the most hated man in Irish history.

SECRET organizations were rife in Ireland. The Fenians and the Land League were the two main arteries of thought but, within them and in smaller groups outside of them, other groups fought a sub-rosa battle against English authority. These were the main thorns in the side of the English as well as in the side of the factions which sought permanent and peaceful solutions of the Irish question.

James Carey, tall, thin of face and heavily bearded, was sitting in his home one evening, reading. In the kitchen was his wife, and scattered around the small house were his seven children.

A knock came at the door, an almost furtive knock, and Carey went to see who could be calling on him at this late hour. It was nearly nine and very few Irishmen roamed the streets of Dublin so late in times like these. There was no telling what might happen to an innocent pedestrian.

The man who stood on the threshhold was an imposing character. A certain esoteric light seemed to shine in his blue eyes.

"I am Walsh," he said succinctly, and stepped inside past the gangling form of Carey, who made no effort to stop him.

The visitor glanced around the room, stepped over to the open kitchen door and looked inside. Mrs. Carey was busy there, unmindful of the man who stood watching her. Walsh shut the door softly. Carey's children watched silently, huddled into a scared group.

"Now what would you be wantin', sir?" Carey asked, after the man had returned into the center of the room.

"I would be wantin' to talk to you, James Carey," Walsh said slowly, "about matters that are secret and having to do with the future of our country."

"We'll be going upstairs, Mr. Walsh," Carey said, frowning.

Walsh nodded his approval of this expediency. He heard the kitchen door open and close and a babble of young voices; then the soft voice of Carey's wife.

"Now, be quiet," she said, "sure 'tis not for the likes of your ears. 'Tis your father's business. Mind, not a word."

Carey smiled as he stepped into an upstairs bedroom, followed closely by Walsh.

An hour later, one of the Carey children could stand no longer the curiosity into his father's business. He tip-toed upstairs, put his ear to the closed door of the bedroom. His eyes widened as he listened.

"—and you swear to keep secret all that has been told to you; to guard with your life, upon penalty of death if you fail, the principles of The Invincibles."

He heard his father swear, then ran quietly down the stairs to join his brothers and sisters in their innocent amusements below.

The next day Mrs. Carey approached her husband. "James," she asked, "what would be The Invinvibles. Denis said something this mornin' about it. He was listening last night, and his tongue was loose to me. I thrashed him good. What is it all about?"

"Mary," James Carey said. "It be nothing so far as you need worry your pretty head. But be mum. It is not a matter for general knowledge."

That was in November, 1881. On May 6, 1882, Lord Frederick Cavendish and Thomas Henry Burke were murdered by a group of assassins in Phoenix Park. The name of The Invincibles does not come into the story again until the Spring of 1883, and then only from the lips of James Carey.

The investigation into the Phoenix Park murders came to naught. The police suspected, and so did everyone generally, that the crime had been committed by members of the Fenian group, but the organization itself was not blamed. It could not be held legally responsible for a what a radical fringe in its membership might possibly do.

Chief Superintendent Mallon reluctantly closed the case as one of those crimes which might never be solved.

ON THE evening of November 27, 1882, Denis J. Field limped into the police station nearest Phoenix Park. Blood covered his face and dripped over his clothing. He was a sorry sight, and a doctor was called immediately to take care of him.

Field told the authorities a strange story, but similar to one they had heard before, on the night of May 6 to be exact.

Three days later, before Magistrate John Adye Curran, one of the Divisional Justices of Dublin, Field told his story again, this time to the man who was eventually to break the case of the double murder in Phoenix Park .

"I was walking along the main road in the Park," Field said, still wincing from the pain of the many knife wounds in his slight body. "It was sort of dark, but I had walked through there many times and I had nothing to fear.

"I came near the shrubs just past the recreation field when it seemed a hundred men jumped out from behind upon me. They had knives in their hands and one man cried, 'Ah, you villian!' as he jumped at me.

"I could not fight against such odds, and in a few minutes I was already weak from loss of blood. I lay still, hoping that they would think I was dead and leave me be. The trick worked and they left as quickly as they had appeared. Then I got me to the police station."

"Did you recognize any of the men?" Curran asked.

"That I· didn't, your honor. It was too dark."

"Can you think of any reason why you would be attacked?"

Field shook his head. "Perhaps, Your Honor. I was a juror in the Casey murder trial, and Casey was convicted. That might be it."

Curran nodded. "We'll do everything we can, Mr. Field, and thank you for coming to me."

After the man had left, Curran thought long and hard about the Field stabbing. One angle that stuck in his mind was the similarity of attack in the Field case and the murders of Cavendish and Burke. It pointed to one thing; that it might have been the same gang, perhaps a secret organization that English spies had not been able to uncover, or had even heard of.

Then the three words: "Ah, you villian!" He recalled seeing these same words in a report on the Phoenix Park murders. Perhaps that was a lead. He would find out.

First of all, the Magistrate asked that his order to investigate Field's attack be broadened to include a re-opening of the Phoenix Park murders. This was granted to him and he began his investigations with the help of the previous investigator, Chief Mallon and a Constabulary aide, A. E. Horne.

They had something more tenuous to go on, and with the attack on a private citizen, having no ties with the authorities, it was possible that witnesses to either of the attacks might come forward. It was not a question of patriotism now.

Magistrate Curran's analysis was correct. Mallon, in his first investigation, had reported a cyclist near the crime who had heard one of the men cry out, "Ah, you villian!"

Curran talked with the man again but found out nothing more than Mallon had learned, yet it was a systematic beginning and it would not hurt to go over what was already known.

The Fenians were suspected. In fact, the police had plenty of suspects but not one whit of evidence that would hold water in court. It was time to do something drastic.

Curran decided on a bold stroke. He would call each and every one of the suspects before him and interrogate them. Out of the several dozen, perhaps one would break.

It was not only a bold stroke, but a decidedly dangerous one. He had no authority, under the English law, to search each suspect for possible hidden weapons as he or she entered the court room. He could only take precautions that would protect himself from any attack. He armed himself and never went out or remained without a police guard at all times.

As he questioned each suspect, he kept his hand always on a cocked revolver in his pocket.

MANY times during the ensuing investigation, Curran was ready to quit. He was getting nowhere. The attitude of the Irish people was decidedly unfavorable toward English authority. Only one glimmering of hope entered his investigation. It came from the direction of Robert Farrell, one of the suspects and a leading Fenian.

Curran's questions to Farrell were put in such a way that they gave Farrell the impression that all the supposed facts had been proven. Farrell acted surprised, and his manner at the inquiry indicated that he suspected that some one had turned informer.

Curran closed the inquiry, released all the suspects, and settled back to wait and hope.

He did not have long to wait. A message came from Inspector Kavanaugh of the Constabulary. Farrell had visited that police official and, being certain in his own mind that some one had turned informer, he had made a statement giving full details of the conspiracy.

Curran brought Farrell before

him. The Fenian repeated his statement and signed a transcript of it, saying that he had not wanted to do it, but that he wasn't going to be made the goat.

Thus Curran came into possession of all the names of the participants in the double murders at Phoenix Park. The men responsible were Joseph Brady, Patrick Delaney, Thomas Caffrey, Timothy Kelly, Michael Fagan, Joseph Hanlon, Daniel Curley, Joseph Smith and *James Carey*. Also on his list was James FitzHarris, a cabman, and Michael Kavanaugh, the man who had driven the assassins to and away from the scene of the murders.

Now, Curran needed corroboration of Farrell's statement. The evidence of an informer would not stand up in court. But, with definite, though uncorroborated, proof of the gang's conspiracy, Curran found it easier to handle witnesses, and to find them. Tongues were loosened under pressure and confirmation of the conspiracy was established. It remained for James Carey to put the clincher on the Crown's case against The Invincibles.

Carey came forth and offered to turn King's evidence after several witnesses had placed Curley, Fagan and himself near the scene of the crime in damning testimony that left no loophole.

Carey's testimony sent Curley, Fagan, Kelly, Brady and Caffrey to the gallows. Delaney won a commutation of his death sentence, and, with four other conspirators, was doomed to spend the remainder of his life in prison at hard labor.

Seven others received jail terms in variance to the importance of their participation in the crimes to eliminate certain undesirable English officials and those unsympathetic to the Irish cause.

A list of the intended victims had been given to Carey by Walsh at the time of their first meeting in 1881. Carey surrendered this list at the time he informed on his co-conspirators. Heading the roster was the name of "Buckshot" Forster, the much hated predecessor of Lord Cavendish. But the efficiency of The Invincibles in carrying out their avowed purpose was not as good as their secrecy. They made more than two dozen attempts on Forster's life without once succeeding in harming him.

In return for his services, Carey was given 100 pounds and went free—to become the most hated man in Irish history.

IN THE Summer of 1883 the steamer *Kinfauns Castle* set out from the port of Dartmouth, on the Dorset coast, bound for Cape Town, Africa. Among the passengers was an Irishman with a heavy beard that cascaded over his upper chest like a jet scarf. He had boarded the vessel with his wife

and seven children and was listed as "James Powers" on the roster of passengers.

After the steamer had been at sea for several days and the passengers had begun to accustom themselves to life on shipboard, the usual acquaintanceships were struck up. Powers took an interest in a tall, red-faced, unmistakable Irishman whose booming brogue was curiously interwoven with unfamiliar American idioms.

Powers engaged him in conversation one day as they leaned over the rail on the top deck, and introduced himself.

"Howdy, pardner!" replied the tall man, extending his hand. "I'm Patrick O'Donnell. Ever make this trip before?"

"No; this is my first sea voyage," replied Powers. "Can't say I like it much, either—"

"Oh, you get used to it—the water all around, I mean."

"You're a seasoned traveler, I take it?"

O'Donnell chuckled. "No, but I've crossed to America and back. It's a fine country. I had some silver mines there. Then I got into the Civil War—you can't keep us Irish out of a good fight, y'know! —and now I'm going to try my luck in South Africa . . . "

Their casual acquaintance blossomed into a strong friendship aboard the *Kinfauns Castle*. O'Donnell had planned to settle in Cape Town, but Powers, who was bound for Natal, persuaded him that the latter city offered more opportunities to a man of O'Donnell's adventurous spirit. O'Donnell thought well of the idea, and at Cape Town, the last port of call of the *Kifauns Castle,* he bought a ticket to Natal aboard the steamer *Melrose*. After leaving the ticket office, Powers and O'Donnell did the sights of Capetown, and made the rounds of the groggeries.

It was the latter part of July when the *Melrose* cleared the harbor of Cape Town. Powers and O'Donnell were standing at the ship's bar. Powers, holding half a glass of ale in his hand, was laughing at a joke of O'Donnell's.

That joke was fatal.

O'Donnell told it in an effort to cover up a sudden coolness toward his ship-board friend. Outwardly, he showed no lessening of his comradery with Powers, but inwardly he was seething. But Powers could not know of O'Donnell's qualities as the champion poker player in the wild mining camps of the American West, where a man had to appear calm even when staring at a fistful of aces, or filling an "inside straight."

Powers did not know it, but a fellow passenger had shown O'Donnell a picture shortly after the *Melrose* had pulled away from the dock. It was the picture of an arch villian, hated by the Irish the world over—James Carey.

And Powers was James Carey!

Passengers sitting out on deck and in the smoking salon, where the bar was located, suddenly were aware of the sound of loud voices from the two men at the bar. Seemingly, a heated argument was in progress, and they paid no attention. Then all at once a shot rang out. Powers, or Carey, crumpled to the floor, showering himself with his half-consumed ale. A revolver fell with a dull thud beside the body.

O'Donnell stared for a long minute at the dying man, then calmly announced to the excited crowd that he was guilty of the murder. He requested that the captain be summoned from the bridge to place him in custody.

THEY hanged Patrick O'Donnell at Newgate Prison, England, on December 17, 1883. *The Irish World,* published in New York, raised $50,000 from Irish folk all over the United States for his defense, and sent one of the most eminent lawyers of New York to help his London solicitors.

O'Donnell's plea of self defense failed to save him, nor could the prayers of the Irish all over the world bring a hoped-for divine intervention.

But as he dangled at the rope's end, all Ireland hailed him as a national hero for ending the career of James Carey, thus closing a bloody chapter in Irish history and cleaning the slate of the last of "The Invincibles".

The Cobra Woman

(*Continued from page* 116)

The verdict was death by hanging. She has appealed.

SO FRAU Martha Marek sits today in a small, chill cell at Vienna Police Headquarters, a still comely blonde of forty, awaiting word whether and when she is to mount the gallows.

A few feet down the corridor outside her dank prison, a clock relentlessly records the fleeting minutes.

She appears stoical enough, unaffected by remorse and unconcerned that her list of crimes reads like some fictional horror-tale of the Dark Ages.

And as this story goes to press, she may be told that Adolph Hitler has rejected her appeal and has ordered her hanged forthwith. If so, she will be the first woman to mount the gallows, in what was once Austria, in almost 40 years. But perhaps Herr Hitler will prefer to order her head chopped off by a Nazi axman in evening clothes, his favorite form of execution.

The Forbidden Secrets of Sex are Daringly Revealed!

AWAY with false modesty! At last a famous doctor has told *all* the secrets of sex in frank, daring language. No prudish beating about the bush, no veiled hints, but TRUTH, blazing through 576 pages of straightforward facts.

Love is the most *magnificent ecstasy* in the world... know how to hold your loved one . . . don't glean half-truths from unreliable sources . . . why not let Dr. H. H. Rubin tell you *what to do* and *how to do it!*

MORE THAN 100 VIVID PICTURES

The 106 illustrations leave *little* to the imagination... know how to overcome physical mismating . . . know what to do on your wedding night to avoid the torturing results of ignorance.

Everything pertaining to sex is discussed in daring language. All the things you have wanted to know about your sex life, information about which other books only vaguely hint, is yours at last.

Some will be offended by the amazing frankness of this book and its vivid illustrations, but the world has no longer any use for prudery and false modesty.

Don't be a *slave* to ignorance and fear. Enjoy the rapturous delights of perfect love life!

Lost love . . . scandal . . . divorce . . . can often be prevented by knowledge. Only the ignorant pay the *awful penalties* of wrong sex practices.

ATTRACT THE OPPOSITE SEX!

Know *how to enjoy* the thrilling experiences that are your birthright . . . . know how to attract the opposite sex.

There is no longer any need to pay the *awful price* for one moment of bliss. Read the scientific pathological facts told so bravely by Dr. Rubin. The chapters on venereal disease are alone worth the price.

What Every Man Should Know

The Sexual Embrace
Secrets of the Honeymoon
Mistakes of Early Marriage
Homosexuality
Venereal Diseases
Can Virility Be Regained?
Sexual Starvation
Glands and Sex Instinct
To Gain Greater Delight
The Truth About Abuse

What Every Woman Should Know

Joys of Perfect Mating
What to Allow a Lover to do
Intimate Feminine Hygiene
Prostitution
Birth Control
How to Attract and Hold Men
Sexual Slavery of Women
Essentials of Happy Marriage
The Sex Organs

EUGENICS AND SEX HARMONY

FORMERLY ~~$5.00~~ NOW ONLY $2.98

STATE AGE WHEN ORDERING

FREE! Amazing New Book on Natural Method of Birth Control

New BIRTH CONTROL FACTS

Away with artificial devices! Nature offers a dependable, healthful method of controlling conception as recently proven in startling scientific tests. The famous Ogino-Knaus theory of rhythmic birth control is explained in detail and includes a complete table of fertile periods. This book is FREE with orders for "Eugenics and Sex Harmony."

PIONEER PUBLICATIONS, Inc. Radio City, 1270 Sixth Ave., N. Y. C.

PIONEER PUBLICATIONS, INC.
Dept. 1144, 1270 Sixth Ave., New York, N. Y.

Please send me, "Eugenics and Sex Harmony" in plain wrapper. I will pay the postman $2.98 (plus postage) on delivery. If I am not completely satisfied, I can return the book within five days and the entire purchase price will be refunded immediately. Also send me FREE OF CHARGE, your book, "New Birth Control Facts."

Name. . . . . Age. . . . . . .

Address. . . . .

Foreign orders 15 shillings in advance

The Fiction House Press Replica Line is available at www.FictionHousePress.com

www.ingramcontent.com/pod-product-compliance
Lightning Source LLC
LaVergne TN
LVHW091005080826
845145LV00003B/1133